The Visitor
A Gracie Island Christmas
Leigh Fenty

Copyright © 2023 by Leigh Fenty

All rights reserved.

No portion of this book may be reproduced in any form without written permission from the publisher or author, except as permitted by U.S. copyright law.

Chapter One

"Not much gets by you, Chief."

It was Saturday morning, and Jasper was preparing to make his weekly run to the lighthouse. He'd picked up Bo's grocery order last night. And Jack had an order from the hardware store. The weather was clear even though it was late November.

Winters on Gracie Island were rainy and dreary. But Jasper loved it. It was all he knew and he wouldn't trade it for anything. Thanksgiving was five days away and it'd be Christmas before they knew it. Then a few months later spring would hit. Which would bring more rain. But spring was different. The rain came in squalls which blew through and were followed by high clouds and blue skies. Jasper could think of nothing more beautiful than rain falling with the sun shining overhead. But being November. They probably wouldn't see the sun for a while.

Jensen had been coming with Jasper on his Saturday runs for the last year or so. At first, intermittently. But for the last six months, he'd come every week. He was five and a half and loved accompanying his father on what he presumed was official sheriff's business.

Jasper leaned on the counter and sipped his coffee while Poppie fed Gracie. The baby waved her hands and kicked her feet. She was recently introduced to solid foods and she wasn't yet sure what she thought about it.

"Your daughter's hungry, Poppie."

"She's impatient. Reminds me of someone."

"Yourself?"

She smiled at him. "There are two impatient people in this kitchen. And I'm not one of them."

"Hmm. Seems to me you couldn't wait for me to get out of the shower this morning."

She laughed. "That had nothing to do with being impatient."

"Well, I did build the shower for two. You could've joined me."

Tucker came running into the room. For the last several months, he only had one speed. Full.

Jasper picked him up as he ran by. "Slow down there, son. Where are you headed?"

"Hungry."

He'd also started communicating in single words. "Hungry for what?"

Tucker pointed at the box of Lucky Charms. "Charms."

"No. You just had breakfast an hour ago. You can have some grapes."

Tucker considered the choice. "Grapes."

"Grapes, please, Dad?"

Tucker frowned. "Grapes."

Jasper looked at Poppie. "Is it normal for him to go from talking in sentences to reverting back to one word?"

"Dr. Hannigan says it's a phase. He's not worried about it."

Jasper took the grapes from the refrigerator, then cut several of them into quarters and put them in a bowl. "Go sit at the table."

Tucker took his grapes and climbed up next to Gracie, who was in an infant seat sitting on the table. "Hi, Gracie. Want a grape?"

Jasper shook his head. "What the hell?"

Poppie laughed. "A phase." She looked at Tucker. "Thank you for offering to share. But Gracie can't eat grapes yet."

Tucker shrugged and popped a piece of grape in his mouth. "Yum."

Jensen came into the room. "When are we going, Dad?"

Jasper finished his coffee. "Right now. Are you ready?"

Jensen nodded. "Yes, sir, Chief."

Jasper kissed Tucker and Gracie's heads, then kissed Poppie. "See you in a few hours."

"Be safe."

"Always."

"Hmm."

"The only time I've ever had trouble on that road was when you were with me." He rubbed his right shoulder at the memory of their lighthouse road adventure. "Worst and best day of my life."

"Go on so you can get back here. I miss you already."

He blew her a kiss. "Love you, Penelope."

"Love you too, Deputy."

After getting Jensen into his car seat, Jasper drove to the fork and turned onto Lighthouse Road. It cut through the island right through the middle of the ten square miles of sand, brush, and groves of red oak, holly, and aspens. There were only two residences on the road. Bo and Emily Redford lived about halfway to the lighthouse. And Jack Anderson and his wife Bindy lived at the end of it. Jack was the lighthouse caretaker, and he lived where the island's most severe weather came in off the ocean. But it seemed they loved it and had been living there for twenty-five years.

When an animal ran across the road, Jasper stepped on the brakes. There were no native animals on the island. A few rodents came over on boats and then escaped and multiplied. But the animal that just ran across the road wasn't a rodent.

Jensen leaned forward in his seat. "What's wrong with that horse, Dad?"

"That wasn't a horse." Jasper pulled over to the side of the road, then got out of the vehicle and let Jensen out. He grabbed his shotgun from the back of the Bronco.

"Are you going to shoot the funny-looking horse, Dad?"

"No, son. I'm not going to shoot it. Come on. Stay close."

Jensen, unlike his mother, generally did what his father told him to do. Especially when they were out in the wilds. So he took hold of the edge of Jasper's pocket and tried to keep up with his father's long strides.

When they came over a small rise, the animal was standing across the clearing, looking at them. He was big with a huge set of antlers, and he was wearing a bright red halter. Jasper stopped walking, and Jensen whispered. "What is it?"

"It's a reindeer."

"Whoa. Cool."

"Shhh. We don't want to spook it."

"What's it doing here?"

"Jensen. Quiet."

"But Dad?"

"Shhh."

The reindeer continue to stare at them and Jasper took a step forward. The reindeer stayed where he was. Jasper wished he had some sort of treat for the animal, then remembered Jensen always had food on him.

"What do you have in your pockets, Junior Deputy?"

Jensen checked his pockets and pulled out a half-eaten sucker.

"No. That won't work."

Jensen took a lick of the sucker, then returned it to his pocket. "I have a granola bar."

"That might do it."

Jensen took the granola bar from his coat pocket. It was squashed and a little warm, but it was still in its wrapper. Jasper took it from him.

"Thanks." He removed the wrapper and tore off a piece. As he prepared to toss it to the reindeer, someone stepped out of the brush.

"I hope you're not planning on feeding that to my reindeer. He's on a very special diet."

Jasper and Jensen both looked at the overweight man, who had long hair and a full beard which were both pure white. Jensen tugged on Jasper's pocket and Jasper put a finger to his lips, then looked at the stranger.

"Sorry. I was trying to get a hand on his halter."

The man whistled, and the reindeer walked over to him. "You don't need to bribe him, Sheriff. You just need to whistle."

Jasper frowned. "So, this is your...reindeer?"

"Yes. I'm afraid he got out of the pen." He hooked a lead line to the reindeer's red halter.

"Pen? Where are you staying?"

"At the place about a half-mile north."

"Sam Jeffer's place?"

"Yes. I was told Sam passed a few years back."

"How long have you been there? And does his son know? He owns it now."

"Young Evan. Of course he knows."

"And how long have you been here? Most visitors check in with the sheriff's office."

"I didn't know it was required. I'm so sorry." He walked up to Jasper, leading the reindeer. "The name is Smith. Chris Smith."

Jasper switched the shotgun to his left hand and shook the man's offered hand. "Chief Goodspeed. And this is my son, Jensen."

"Nice to meet you, Jensen."

Jensen stepped behind Jasper's leg and peaked out. "Is that a real reindeer?"

"Why of course. This is Buck."

Jensen seemed a little disappointed his name wasn't Dasher or Dancer.

Jasper was still confused and very curious about the strange visitor on his island. "How did you get Buck to the island? I'm pretty sure I would've heard about a reindeer catching a ride on the ferry."

Chris laughed heartily and Jasper tried not to compare it to the laugh of a 'right jolly ol' elf'.

"I brought them over in a trailer. I'm sure Jake had no idea what was in it."

"Them?"

"Yes. I have seven more back at Sam's place."

Jasper couldn't quite believe what he was hearing. "You have eight reindeer?"

"Yes."

"Why?" The stranger was odd, as was the whole situation.

Chris laughed again. "Well, just look at him. They're magnificent creatures."

"Okay." Jasper looked at the reindeer again. It was quite impressive. And it was looking at him with eyes that seemed almost human like. *Was the reindeer mocking him?* Jasper shook his head to clear it.

Chris ran a hand down the reindeer's nose. "I should get him back now."

"Right. Of course. Do you need help?"

Chris waved a hand. "No. I'll just cut through the brush. We'll be fine."

"Nice to meet you, Mr. Smith. Welcome to Gracie Island."

"Thank you, Jasper."

Jasper watched as the man disappeared into the brush with Buck the reindeer, then scratched his head. "Did I tell him my name was Jasper?"

"No, Dad. But he knows everybody's names."

"Why?"

"Because he's Santa Claus."

Jasper took Jensen's hand and headed for the Bronco. "No, honey, he isn't. He's just a man who happens to own eight reindeer."

"Dad. He's Santa Claus."

"Come on. We need to go see Bo."

They returned to the Bronco and Jasper waited for Jensen to buckle himself into his carseat before heading down the road. He was curious about Mr. Chris Smith and was anxious to see if Bo knew anything about him.

When he pulled up to Bo's house, Jasper honked the horn twice to let him and Emily know he was there. Not that they didn't hear him driving up the gravel road. Jasper was pretty much their only visitor and he came every Saturday. But still, it was the polite thing to do.

Jasper got out and opened the door for Jensen, who scrambled out and ran to see the animals. Bo had horses, goats, and chickens, and they were the highlight of the trip for Jensen. After a few minutes, Bo came onto the porch.

"Sorry, Chief, I was finishing up my lunch."

Jasper opened the back of the Bronco and Bo came to help unload his supplies. They set several boxes on the porch, before Jasper nodded in the direction of Sam Jeffers' place.

"Have you met your new neighbor?"

"Neighbor?"

"Yeah. I just met him. Says his name is Chris Smith."

"Hmm. I haven't seen any activity over there. But I've been sticking pretty close to home. Emily's been down with a cold."

"Oh. Huh."

"You seem concerned. Is there a problem with this Mr. Smith?"

"I don't know. He was friendly enough. A little evasive. But the really strange thing is, he just kind of showed up. I had no idea he was on the island. Or staying at Sam's place."

"Not much gets by you, Chief."

"I know. But Chris Smith did. With eight reindeer."

Bo started laughing. "Damn. You had me going there for a minute."

"No. I'm serious. The man says he has eight reindeer."

Bo shook his head. "He's pulling your leg."

"Maybe. But he has at least one. Jensen and I saw it. Ran right across the road in front of me and we followed it into the brush."

"The hell you say."

Jasper held up a hand. "God's honest truth."

"Well, I guess I should go introduce myself. I've never seen a reindeer."

Jasper nodded. "Just look for the man with a long white beard."

After leaving Bo's, Jasper continued down the road to the Anderson's. When they went over the last incline before dropping down to the beach, Jensen clapped at the sight of the lighthouse. Next to the animals at Bo's, the lighthouse was a favorite part of the trip, too.

"Can we climb it today, Dad?"

"Not today, son. I need to get back to town. Even though he was technically off duty on Saturdays, he didn't like being out of radio range. A mile past the fork, he was unreachable if an emergency came up. Not that there was much that his deputy, Quinn, couldn't handle. He was typically gone for about two hours. But their trek through the brush chasing down a runaway reindeer had used up some of that time.

When Jasper pulled up to the house, Jack was on the front porch. He came to the Bronco and greeted Jasper as he got out, then waved at Jensen in the backseat.

"How you doing today, Chief?"

"Good. I've got your order in the back." They went to the back of the Bronco and started unloading Jack's supplies. "Have you met the man staying at Sam's old place?"

Jack smiled. "Yeah. I bet he's got that detective mind of yours in a spin."

"He's a little odd, right?"

"The fact that he looks like Santa Claus? Or the fact that he has a herd of reindeer?"

Jasper laughed. "Both. So you've seen the reindeer?"

"Only two of them. Damn near ran one over the other day. Scared Bindy half to death."

"Then Chris showed up?"

"Yeah. Damnedest thing. He whistled, and they came right to him."

"Jensen and I saw one a bit ago. It's strange all right."

Jack put a hand on Jasper's shoulder. "Don't let the time of year and the man's sudden appearance on the island mess with your head."

"But eight reindeer?"

"Stranger things have happened around here."

Jasper couldn't think of any, but he agreed with Jack, anyway. "I guess you're right."

"Are you and Jensen going up in the lighthouse today?"

"No. I've got to get back. I'll see you next week."

"See you, Chief. Happy Thanksgiving."

"You too, Jack."

Chapter Two

"Chief Goodspeed, are you flirting with me?"

When Jasper came into the house from walking the dogs, Poppie looked at him. "So, sounds like you guys had quite the adventure today."

He looked at Jensen. "Did you tell your mother all about Mr. Smith?"

Jensen nodded. "And his reindeer."

"Go get washed up for dinner, son. And help Tucker wash his hands."

"Yes, sir."

Jensen ran off and Jasper looked at Poppie. "It was really weird."

She smiled. "I imagine it was. An actual reindeer. Are you sure it wasn't just a deer?"

"Honey, I know the difference between a deer and a reindeer. Even though I've never seen either in person. Or...whatever."

She put her hands on her hips. "You've never been to a zoo? Or just driven through the countryside on the mainland?"

Jasper washed his hands in the kitchen sink. "Why would I?"

"It's a normal thing for people to do."

"I'm from Gracie Island."

"Yes. I know."

He grabbed the towel and dried his hands. "We don't go to the mainland to drive around in the country. And the closest zoo is in Augusta."

She nodded. "Where you lived for two years."

"I was attending the police academy and counting the days until I could come home."

Poppie put her arms around him. "Does this mean our kids are never going to visit a zoo, either?"

"No need, when there are reindeer running loose on the island." He pulled her in for a kiss. "The weirdest thing was, he had long white hair and a full beard."

"The reindeer?"

Jasper scowled. "You're so funny." He moved to the table and sat down with a sigh. "Jensen is convinced the man is Santa Claus."

"Well, I can see why."

Jasper thought about Chris for a moment. "You know how in movies and stuff about Santa Claus, he knows everyone's name?"

"Yes, because he has a list."

"I introduced myself as Chief Goodspeed. But when he left us, he called me Jasper."

Poppie grinned. "Did he ask you if you've been a good boy this year?"

Jasper shook his head. "You're a smart ass tonight."

"I'm sorry." She laughed. "Maybe you can introduce me to Mr. Smith. I'd love to meet him."

"I'm pretty sure you're currently on his naughty list, so maybe you should steer clear."

Poppie went to him and sat on his lap. "Well, if I'm already on the list, then..." she kissed him, but stopped when Jensen and Tanner ran into the kitchen.

Jasper nodded toward the boys. "That's what being naughty will get you."

Tucker came over to them and patted Poppie's leg. "Hungry."

She sighed and kissed Jasper on the forehead. "The boy is hungry."

She stood and Jasper patted her on the rear as she moved away from him. "We'll continue this conversation later."

"You can count on it, my love."

Monday morning, before going to the office, Jasper went by the marina to talk to Jake before the morning ferry left. He boarded the boat and found Jake in the control room. The ferry made four runs a day and mostly carried passengers. But the lower deck was designed to haul a few cars. And apparently, an occasional trailer full of reindeer.

"Morning Chief. Are you headed to the mainland this morning?"

"No. I wanted to ask you about someone who came over within the last week or so."

"Who might that be? Only had regulars this week as far as I can remember."

Jasper rubbed the back of his neck. "You don't remember someone bringing a stock trailer over. Older man." He took a moment. "White beard."

Jake shook his head. "I would've remembered a stock trailer on my ferry."

"That's what I figured."

"Why?"

"Just checking up on someone. Thanks, Jake. I don't want to make you late for your morning run."

"See you around, Chief."

Jasper left the boat and went down one of the docks to an old trawler moored at the end. He heard cursing as he approached the boat.

"Can you keep it down in there? Or do I have to arrest you for swearing in public?"

Lewis stuck his head out the cabin door. "Is it against the law?"

"It is if I say it is."

Lewis laughed. "What are you doing down here this time of day?" He came out on the deck of the boat, then grinned at Jasper. "I heard about your run in with Santa Claus."

"How the hell?"

"When Poppie dropped the kids off with Sarah. She told us all about it."

Jasper stepped onto the boat and sat on a wooden bench. "It was strange."

"I bet. It's not every day you get to meet Santa Claus."

"And it keeps getting stranger. Jake doesn't remember bringing over a stock trailer."

"Filled with reindeer?"

"Filled with anything. You'd think he'd remember a trailer, right? Bo's the only one in town with a horse trailer. And he hasn't used it in years."

"So, you think Chris Kringle and his reindeer just appeared on the island?"

"No."

Lewis moved his tool box and sat down. "Jake forgot or, somehow, didn't notice...a trailer full of reindeer." He grinned. "Did you actually see eight reindeer?"

"No. I only saw one. But he'd still need a trailer. Even for one."

"Unless they...flew in."

Jasper got to his feet. "I'm going to go now."

"Let's meet up for lunch. This is a crap job and I'm going to need a break in a couple of hours."

Jasper stepped onto the dock. "Sure."

"We can write our Christmas wish lists."

Jasper flipped Lewis off over his shoulder as he walked away. The ferry was pulling out when he passed by it and he gave Jake a wave, then continued to his Bronco. He drove the half-mile to the sheriff's office and parked in front of the building.

When Jasper came into the station, Maisy smiled at him. "Good morning, sweetheart."

"Morning, Maisy."

"There's someone in your office." She went to the coffeemaker and poured a cup of coffee.

"Who?"

Maisy shrugged. "He's not local." She handed Jasper the coffee.

"Thank you." He took a sip, then went to his office door. When he opened it, he found Chris Smith looking at the photos on the bookshelf. It'd taken him a while to make his father's old office his own. But with Poppie's help, it now better reflected him instead of James Goodspeed.

"Mr. Smith?"

Chris turned and gave Jasper a smile. "Good morning, Chief."

"What can I help you with?" Jasper went to his desk and sat down and Chris moved to a chair in front of the desk.

"I came to apologize."

"For what?" Jasper took another sip of coffee, then set his cup down.

"For not checking in with you when I got to your island. I didn't know that was the protocol."

"Right. Well, I guess you wouldn't. Don't worry about it."

"I understand why you'd want to know if a stranger was in town. You need to keep your people safe."

Jasper cocked his head. "I'm assuming I don't need to worry about you in that regard."

Chris chuckled. "Of course not. I pose no danger."

"Good to know. Where are you from, Mr. Smith?"

"Please call me Chris."

Jasper nodded as he noticed Chris was dressed in a red flannel shirt, with black pants and boots. He had a green wool stocking cap in his hand. "Where are you from, Chris?"

"Up north."

"Canada?"

"Sure."

Jasper wanted to pin it down exactly but was afraid of what Chris might say, so he let it go. "You said you came over on the ferry."

"Yes, that's correct."

Jasper leaned back in his chair. "When exactly?"

Chris smiled. "Are you interrogating me, Chief Goodspeed?"

"No. Sorry. Force of habit." He leaned forward and rested his forearms on the desk.

"How's your father?"

"My father?"

"The ex-chief?"

Jasper raised an eyebrow. "Do you know my father?"

Chris got to his feet. "Just making conversation. I saw his picture there on the bookshelf. You have quite a family."

Jasper glanced at the bookshelf. "Thank you."

"Well, I should go. I don't like to leave the boys alone too long."

"By boys you mean…?"

"My reindeer."

"Right." Jasper got to his feet and walked Chris to the door. "Have a good day, Chris."

Chris went out the door, then waved at Maisy on the way through the lobby. "You take care, Maisy."

Jasper waited until Chris was gone before going out to Maisy. "Did you tell him your name was Maisy?"

"Of course, honey. How else would he know?"

Jasper took a breath. "Right."

"Are you okay?"

"Yeah. Mr. Smith just gives me the creeps."

She shook her head. "Nonsense. He seems like a very nice man. Quite friendly."

"Jolly?"

"I suppose. Are you sure you're okay, sweetheart?"

"Yeah. I'll be in my office." He returned to the office and went to look at the pictures on the bookshelf. There was one picture of James. But he wasn't in uniform. He was standing on the beach holding a fish. Which in no way indicated he was Chief Deputy on the island for years.

Jasper returned to his desk and called Poppie, who was stocking the bar at The Sailor's Loft. When she answered, she sounded winded.

"This is Poppie."

He leaned back in his chair. "Hey, honey."

"Duke? I told you not to call me here."

"Wow. I'd rather you had any other man in town calling you besides Duke."

"Why are you calling? Shouldn't you be busy serving and protecting?"

"This is Gracie Island."

"Oh, right. What can I do for you?"

He sat up straight in his chair. "Hmm. Ask me that question again tonight. After the kids are in bed."

"Chief Goodspeed, are you flirting with me?"

He smiled. "Always. How soon will you be done there?"

"I'll be done a lot quicker if I had some help from a handsome and strong Chief Deputy."

"I'll see if I can find one."

"There are a lot of really heavy cases of alcohol here."

He grinned. "I'll be there in thirty minutes."

"Bring your muscles."

Jasper made a few phone calls, and checked for emails from the Sheriff's department on the mainland, then left the office. He told Maisy he'd be at the Loft, then on the radio. But he might be out of range for an hour or so in a while. The radio signal was only good within about a five mile radius of the station.

He parked in front of The Sailor's Loft and rang the bell on the mast three times before going inside. He was greeted by Aunt Peg.

"Hey, honey. Are you here for a late breakfast or an early lunch?"

"Neither. I came to see the three most beautiful women on Gracie Island. Is Mom in the kitchen?"

"Yes. She's baking bread."

Jasper raised an eyebrow. "Is she upset about something?"

"No. It's just Sunday."

Baking bread was Kat's go to stress reliever. But Sunday's, Tuesdays, and Fridays, she baked bread for the restaurant. He headed for the kitchen.

Kat looked up from kneading a ball of dough. "Good morning, sweetheart. Are you here for breakfast?"

"No. I ate at home." He perched on a stool and picked up a muffin. "I'll take one of these, though."

"What's on your mind, son?"

"Nothing. I just came to say hi. I'm going to help Poppie with the order."

She cocked her head at him. "Something's bothering you."

He unwrapped his muffin, then took a bite before responding. "It's this new guy in town."

"There's a new guy in town?"

"Yeah. I ran into him Saturday on my way to see Bo and Emily."

"He was on Lighthouse Road?"

"Yeah. Him and his reindeer."

Kat stopped kneading her dough. "Reindeer?"

"Yeah. Weird, right?"

"A reindeer on Gracie Island is unusual."

She wasn't nearly as curious as Jasper expected her to be. "Unusual? It's damn strange."

"I'm sure the man has a good reason for being here with a reindeer."

Jasper stood. "What possible reason could he have?"

Kat laughed. "Poppie was right. You're totally freaked out by Mr. Chris Smith."

"Dammit. My wife has a big mouth."

"Well, it's not every day her husband and son meet Santa Claus."

Chapter Three

"How'd I become the bad guy?"

Jasper found Poppie in the storeroom behind the bar. "Why don't you just print a front-page story in the Lighthouse Courier? Chief Goodspeed meets Santa Claus. It'd probably sell a lot of papers."

Poppie smiled at him. "The paper is free." They left the storeroom and Jasper sat on a stool in front of the bar. Poppie reached for his hand. "I only told Lewis."

"And my mother."

Poppie laughed. "She thought it was hilarious."

"I'm taking you out there."

"To meet Santa?"

"As soon as we finish putting away the order."

She clapped her hands. "Yay. Can't wait. We need to bring Tucker, though."

"Why?"

"He's being…Tucker today. I was going to collect him and Gracie and leave Jensen, because he wants to stay with Micah. But Sarah will be fine keeping Gracie while we go meet…" Jasper squinted at her. "…the new guy in town."

They spent an hour taking care of the order and stocking the bar for the night. Today being Monday, it'd be open from three to ten. Mondays were slow and they had shorter hours. Poppie worked the bar two days a week on Tuesday and Wednesday from one to six. She loved it, and it gave her a chance to get out and have adult conversations for a few hours a week. She was also the bar manager and took care of ordering and stocking the bar. Occasionally, if Mark needed a night off, Jasper would cover for him. Kat and Peg were both capable of working the bar, too, in an emergency.

When Poppie was satisfied the bar was ready for the evening business, she and Jasper went to the Bronco, then headed for Lewis and Sarah's place. They'd move to town after the hurricane that swept over the island a few months ago. The once in a lifetime storm, flooded their house and left it uninhabitable until Lewis would be able to put some serious work into it. But the whole event was traumatic for Sarah and she told Lewis she'd never be able to live in the house again. Even if he got it back to what it once was. They now lived in a three bedroom house a block over from Kat and James.

Sarah came out with Gracie in her arms, and Matty and Tucker followed her down the steps. Tucker ran to Poppie when he saw her, and she picked him up with a groan. Tucker was a big almost three-year-old, so groaning was a natural part of picking him up. At least for Poppie. Jasper didn't have a problem toting his son around.

"Hey big boy." She kissed him on the cheek.

He put his hands on either side of her face. "Home."

Poppie smiled at Sarah. "Would you mind keeping Gracie for just a while longer?" She glanced at Jasper. "We're going to meet…Mr. Smith."

"Oh man, I want to go." Sarah grinned at Jasper. "It's not every day you get to meet the man." Jasper frowned and she patted his arm. "Of course I'll watch her. I can keep the little Tuckster if you need me to."

Poppie adjusted her grip on Tucker. "No. We'll take him. He's been a little full of it lately."

Sarah rubbed his back. "You get to meet...a reindeer."

Poppie laughed. "We'll be back soon."

"Have fun. And take a picture. I want to see these reindeer and Mr. Smith."

"I'll try." Poppie still carried her cell phone on her, even though there was no cell service on the island. But she liked having the camera. And she could download the pictures on Jasper's computer at the station. City Hall had the only internet service on the island, courtesy of a tower on top of the building with a satellite dish.

With Tucker secured in his car seat, Jasper drove out of town to Harper's Fork, then turned on Lighthouse Road. When he got to the road leading to the Jeffers' property, he turned and drove to the house. The house had been empty for six years. Evan Jeffers had no desire to move into his father's old, rundown place. But he hadn't tried to sell it either. So it sat empty. Until now. When they cleared the trees, Poppie gasped at the sight of eight reindeer in the wooden pen.

"Oh my gosh."

"I told you."

"Oh...my gosh."

Jasper turned off the Bronco and got out of the vehicle as Chris came out of the house. He gave Jasper a smile and a wave. Jasper glanced at Poppie, who was now staring at Chris.

He whispered, "Quit staring." He closed his door, then approached the small porch. "Sorry to bother you. My wife wanted to see your reindeer. Hope it's okay we just dropped in."

"Sure. Of course." Chris did his 'bowl full of jelly' chuckle.

Jasper waved at Poppie and she stepped out of the Bronco, and smiled at Chris. "Hi there."

"Mrs. Goodspeed. Welcome."

She took Tucker from his car seat, then went to stand next to Jasper.

Chris smiled at Tucker. "This must be..." He glanced at Jasper and raised an eyebrow.

"Tucker. Our youngest son."

Tucker looked at Chris and said, "Santa."

Jasper smiled. "Sorry about that."

Chris laughed and stroked his beard. "Don't be. I get that all the time. I bet young Tucker would like to see the reindeer. Let me get some carrots."

He disappeared into the house, and Jasper and Poppie walked to the pen full of eight reindeer.

Poppie shook her head. "I don't believe it. I'm looking at them, and I don't believe it."

Tucker clapped his hands. "Horse."

Poppie patted his back. "Reindeer, honey."

Tucker looked at her. "Horse."

Jasper leaned in to Poppie's ear. "Now do you get why I'm slightly freaked out?"

"Yes."

Chris came up to them with a package of carrots in his hand. He took one from the bag and held it out to Tucker. "Would you like to feed a reindeer?"

Tucker hid his face in Poppie's neck, and she took the carrot from Chris. "Thank you. He's kind of shy." She held out the carrot and one of the reindeer approached her, sniffed the carrot, then took it from her. She laughed. "What's his name?"

"That's Star. He's a bold one. The others look to him to make the first move."

Two more reindeer came to the fence and Poppie fed them each a carrot. "They're so polite."

"That's Regi and Rex. They do everything together."

Buck came for a carrot, then over the next ten minutes, all the reindeer were fed a couple of carrots and Chris identified the rest of them as Bingo, Tuffy, Bright, and Cookie. The reindeer appeared to be gentle and well-trained. And it was obvious Chris loved them.

When they moved away from the pen, Poppie smiled at Chris. "Thank you for letting us meet them. They're awesome."

"My pleasure."

Despite Chris' hospitality, Jasper was still uncertain about the mysterious stranger. "How long are you staying, Chris?"

"Not long. Just until the holidays."

"I expect once word gets out about your reindeer, you'll get some visitors."

He nodded. "That's fine. I like visitors. And so do the boys. I'll need to keep stocked up on carrots."

"Right. But if it gets to be too much. Just let me know. I'll tell folks to leave you alone."

"I'll be sure to do that."

Jasper glanced at Poppie. "We should get back. Thanks again."

"Come any time."

Jasper and Poppie got back in the Bronco with Tucker, and as they drove away, Tucker said, "Santa."

Jasper glanced back at him. "He was barely two last Christmas. There's no way he knows who Santa is."

Poppie patted Jasper's thigh. "He must've heard Jensen talking about Chris."

"And he made the connection? I don't think so." Jasper looked at her. "You have to think this is as weird as I do."

Poppie nodded. "Yeah, it's weird."

"So what the hell is going on?"

She shrugged. "Obviously, it's just our imaginations working overtime. The time of year. The fact he looks like…" She shook her head. "It's Santa Claus, Jasper."

"Okay. Let's suspend reality for a moment and say there is a man who flies around the world every Christmas Eve, delivering presents to good little girls and boys. What the hell is he doing on Gracie Island?"

"On vacation before his big night?"

"Why here? Why not Florida? Or California? How about Hawaii?"

"Maybe those places are too warm for him. And maybe he wants to be incognito. And transporting eight reindeer to Hawaii would be quite an undertaking. Unless, of course…"

Jasper sighed. "Are we really having this conversation?"

Poppie laughed. "Whoever he is. And whatever he's doing, he says he'll be gone before the holidays."

"Right before Christmas?"

"This is so weird."

When they pulled into Sarah's driveway, Jensen and Micha ran to the Bronco. When Poppie got out, Jensen looked up at her.

"Did you see him, Mom? Did you see Santa?"

"I met Chris Smith and his reindeer. They're very cool."

Jensen crossed his arms and scowled at her. "I thought at least you'd believe he was real."

Poppie knelt down and hugged him. "I believe that you believe, and that's proof enough for me."

Jensen smiled. "Thank you, Mom." He frowned at Jasper, then ran off.

Jasper shook his head. "How'd I become the bad guy?"

Poppie went to him and gave him a hug, then whispered in his ear. "Because you don't believe in Santa Claus."

"Neither do you."

"But I don't advertise it."

"Hmm. I fully support believing in the Santa Claus myth. But that doesn't mean I have to believe the man living in Sam Jeffers' place is him."

"Okay, Mr. Scrooge."

"I'm not a Scrooge. You've spent six Christmases with me. You know I love Christmas."

She patted his chest. "Yes. You do. You're not a Scrooge. I'm sorry."

"Thank you."

Sarah came out of the house with Gracie and handed her to Jasper. "How'd it go?"

Jasper shook his head and went to put Gracie in her car seat.

Poppie took Sarah's arm. "It appears Santa is vacationing on Gracie Island."

Jasper joined them again. "If your husband calls, tell him I'm ready for lunch as soon as I take Poppie and the kids home."

"He already called and asked where you were. Only he wasn't that polite about it. I'll call him back and tell him to meet you…"

"At the deli in thirty."

She looked at Poppie. "Did you get pictures?"

Poppie took out her phone and pulled up the pictures of the reindeer.

Sarah looked through them all, then handed the phone back to her. "No pictures of Santa?"

"I figured that might be rude. And...I don't know. Maybe he'd think I was stealing his soul or something."

Jasper took Poppie's arm. "That's indigenous native tribes who have never seen the white man before."

She shrugged. "It would've been rude."

He steered her toward the Bronco. "Bye, Sarah."

"Bye guys. I'm going to go bake some Christmas cookies."

Jasper frowned. "Christmas is five weeks away."

"I'm suddenly in the holiday spirit. I'll send some home with Jensen."

Chapter Four

"Princess Penny is a drama queen."

After dropping off Poppie and the kids, Jasper drove back into town and found Lewis sitting in front of the grocery store with an order of tacos and a large drink. Jasper sat across the picnic table from him.

"You didn't wait for me?"

"It's two o'clock, man. I'm starving."

"Sorry. I got stuck feeding reindeer."

Lewis grinned. "So Sarah said. She told me Poppie took pictures, too."

"Yeah. And now your wife is home baking Christmas cookies."

"Cool. I love Christmas cookies."

"Christmas is a month away."

"It's never too early to eat Christmas cookies."

Jasper stood. "I'm going to go order something. How are the tacos today? Who's working the deli?"

"Rita. So they're good."

Jasper nodded and went inside the grocery store. The deli was well-stocked and had a lot to offer. Rita greeted him with a smile. On the days she worked the food was always consistently good. On her day's off, though, good food was hit and miss.

"Good afternoon, Chief."

"Afternoon, Rita. Can you make me three supreme tacos with extra onions and some beans at the bottom of it all?"

"Coming right up. Will you tell your mother we got her turkeys in?"

"Will do."

He took his three tacos and a large iced tea and went back outside to Lewis. The weather was still holding, which was odd for this time of year. Generally by late November, there was no sitting outside to eat.

Lewis looked up at the partly cloudy sky. "This fall weather in late November is weird."

"The weather has been off since the hurricane. But it won't last. There's supposed to be some weather moving in next weekend. And the long-term forecast for December is lots of rain."

"Well, duh. When don't we have a rainy December? Or January and February, for that matter?"

"Along with March, April, and May." Jasper took a bite of a taco and nodded. "Mmm. Good." He finished chewing, then looked at Lewis. "So, are you still thinking about going to Boston for Thanksgiving?"

"No. Too far. Too many kids. Too much everything. Are we still invited to the Loft?"

"Of course. Every year."

Lewis smiled. "I thought maybe you passed my invite off to one of your other brother-in-laws."

"If I had another brother-in-law, maybe. I can't believe you even considered leaving us this year. Who would I have beaten at the air hockey tournament?"

"It's Mom and Dad. Every year they beg us to come. They've given up on you and Poppie ever showing up."

Jasper shrugged. "I figure it's a lot easier for the two of them to come here than for either of us to haul our kids there."

"Along with the fact, you hate leaving the island."

"That too."

Jasper left the island only when he had to. Once a month, for a meeting with the sheriff in the county seat. And a medical flight once in a while if someone needed services Dr. Hannigan couldn't provide. Or if they had to be hospitalized. Most of the islanders went to the mainland to stock up on groceries. But Jasper liked to shop local. Steadman's had everything they needed and he didn't mind paying a little extra for it.

Jasper finished lunch with Lewis, then spent a few more hours at the office before heading home. As he usually did, he took the dogs to the beach to run around for a few minutes before dinner. He sat on an old wooden bench and watched Jensen play with the dogs in the sand which was still wet from the tide going out.

Their chihuahua, Penny, usually tired out before the bigger dogs, and when she laid down in the sand, Jensen picked her up and brought her to Jasper.

"Penny is pooped, Dad."

Jasper took the dog from Jensen and tucked her in his wool jacket. "Thanks, son." Poppie squirmed for a moment, then settled down.

Jensen sat on the bench next to Jasper. "When can I go see all the reindeer, Dad?"

"I don't know. I don't want to bother Mr. Smith too much."

"But Tucker got to see them."

Jasper sighed. "Maybe on my day off."

Jensen jumped to the ground. "Cool!" He ran off to join Sam and Blackjack.

Despite the milder day, it was getting cold now that the sun was almost down. And Jasper was having trouble keeping an eye on Jensen and the dogs in the waning light. With Penny still snuggled in his jacket, he stood and whistled. A few minutes later, Jensen and Blackjack ran to him, and they headed up the sandy path to the house. Sam usually held out for a few more minutes. But he always showed up before they got to the front porch. Jasper told the big dogs to stay on the porch so they could dry off, then took Jensen and Penny inside. Unless someone drove up to the house, which was a rare occurrence, the dogs stayed put. They knew as soon as they were dry, they could come inside to eat.

Poppie smiled at Jasper and Jensen, then came to take Penny from Jasper. "You guys look cold." She snuggled Penny. "And this little one is shivering."

"She's been inside my coat for the last fifteen minutes. She's playing you."

Poppie held Penny up a few inches in front of her face. "Is that right, Princess Penny? Are you trying to get attention?"

Penny wagged her tail and licked the end of Poppie's nose.

Jasper laughed. "Princess Penny is a drama queen."

After dinner, while Poppie bathed the kids and got them ready for bed, Jasper sat on the couch with the paperwork he'd brought home from the office. He hated paperwork. He hated it even more when he had to bring it home with him. Fortunately, Maisy took care of a lot of the day-to-day stuff, leaving only official chief business to Jasper.

When Poppie came in with a plate of Christmas cookies Jensen brought home from his Aunt Sarah, Jasper set the file he was looking at aside and rubbed his eyes.

Poppie put the plate of cookies on the coffee table and sat next to Jasper. "Homework, Chief?"

"Yeah. My favorite. With Thomas out recovering from his surgery, I've had to take on the role of mayor, too."

"When will he be back in his office?"

"Next Monday. He and Maisy will be at Thanksgiving dinner, though."

"And you're taking Wednesday off?"

"Yes. Quinn is working. But I'll be on call on Thanksgiving, and he'll be gone on Friday. He and Amy are going to Nova Scotia to see his parents."

"Well, in six years, you've never had to leave the table on Thanksgiving, so let's hope this isn't the first year you get called out."

Jasper reached for a cookie shaped like a snowman and took a bite. "I've decided to stop trying to figure out who or what Chris Smith is."

Poppie nodded. "Good. Chances are, he's just a nice old man with eight pet reindeer."

"Exactly. Who mysteriously showed up on the island a month before Christmas. Has a name that sounds like Christmas if you say it fast. And knew my name, even though I never told him what it was."

She patted his leg, then handed him another cookie. "Way to let it go, my love."

On Wednesday morning, Jasper wanted to sleep in. He'd be helping his mother set up for dinner tomorrow, but that wasn't until after lunch. He was comfortably enjoying the space between sleep and wakefulness when he was brought fully awake by a sharp jolt to his stomach. He sat up and Jensen rolled off of him.

"Geez, honey!"

"Sorry, Dad. Did I get you in the you know whats?"

Jasper laid back down and closed his eyes as he rubbed his stomach. "No. I'm trying to sleep, kid."

"Can we go see the reindeer today?"

Jasper opened his eyes and looked at Jensen. "Didn't we talk about this already?"

"Yeah. But that was a long time ago. I've been very patient. And you said maybe on your day off."

Jasper smiled. "Yes, you have been very patient. But today I need to help Grandma at the Loft. And you know that maybe means maybe, and not absolutely."

Jensen frowned and dropped down onto Poppie's pillow.

Jasper patted his leg. "*Maybe* on Friday."

Jensen sat back up. "Really?"

"If I'm not too busy. Quinn will be out of town, so I won't have any backup."

"As long as it's a maybe."

"It's a maybe."

Jensen jumped off the bed and ran for the door, running into Poppie coming through it.

"Hey. Slow down. And I told you not to come in here and bother your dad."

"Sorry, Mom."

"Go eat your breakfast. I'll be back in a minute." She came to the bed. "I'm sorry. Did he wake you up?"

"Yes. By doing a pile driver to my gut."

Poppie sat next to him, then moved his hand and kissed the spot underneath it. "Mommy will make it all better."

Jasper took her by the shoulders and pushed her down on the bed. "What else can Mommy do for me?"

She giggled, then kissed him before sitting up. "I can't leave those three alone in the kitchen. Tucker is determined to offer Gracie everything under the sun. It's very sweet that he wants to share, but she's barely eating solids."

"You better go then."

"Are you going to take a shower?"

"Yeah."

"Maybe I'll come in and scrub your back for you."

"From inside the shower or from outside the shower?" When she cocked her head, he nodded. "I know. Kids. How did we ever have more than one?"

He watched her go, then put an arm behind his head. He'd tried not to think about Chris over the last couple of days, and he'd been mostly successful. But now he was thinking of the man spending Thanksgiving alone in Sam's old house. The right thing to do would be to drive out there and invite him to dinner with the family. A third of the town would be there, seeing as the Goodspeeds were related to them all, one way or another. Kat was a direct descendant of Henry Gracie, the original owner of the island. And there had been a Goodspeed in the sheriff's department for four generations. So, one more person would hardly be noticed. Although Jasper suspected that somehow, everyone would notice Chris Smith if he showed up for dinner.

Chapter Five

"Like a bowl full of jelly."

The Sailor's Loft was still open for business on Wednesday, but the customers were being seated in the bar, so Jasper, his father James, and his Uncle Beryl could get the dining room set up for the family dinner on Thursday. It wasn't very busy, as everyone was getting ready for the holiday, but a few of the die-hard regulars came in.

For as long as Jasper could remember, they always arranged the dining room the same way. The tables were put into a large square, with the chairs only on the outside of it. That way, no one had their back to anyone and conversations could be held across the empty space. There was another row of tables to hold the food. Dinner would be set up buffet style with endless amounts of turkey, potatoes, stuffing, fresh bread, and so much more. The hardest part of the day every year was trying to keep Aunt Peg from trying to serve everyone, and keeping his mother out of the kitchen.

The bar would be available if anyone wanted a drink. Mixing drinks usually fell to Jasper and Uncle Beryl. As a recovering alcoholic, James stayed away from the bar, and Poppie usually had her hands full with the kids or helping Kat.

When the men stopped for a moment to rest after forming the square of tables, Jasper decided to broach the subject of inviting Chris to the family dinner. He wouldn't be the only non-family member to attend. Burt, who was a ward of the island, came every year. Burt was mentally challenged, but was able to live alone in the house he grew up in. Everyone in town kept an eye on him and made sure he had enough to eat and that his house remained in good condition. The Redfords and the Andersons were always invited, but only came occasionally. And there was always an open invitation to anyone who had no one else to spend the holiday with.

James looked at Jasper. "What's on your mind, son?" James had been an uninvolved father while Jasper was growing up, and it was only the last few years they'd forged a relationship resembling that of a father and son. But James had always been able to tell when Jasper was debating something in his head.

"I was thinking about asking the new guy staying in Sam's old place to dinner."

"You know all are welcome if they need a place to go."

"Yeah. Still, I thought I should run it by you and Mom."

James laughed. "Your Mom's the boss on Thanksgiving. I've got no say. But I've heard some talk about the man. Is it true he has a few reindeer?"

"Yeah. Eight of them."

"Eight? Just enough to pull a sleigh." He and Beryl started laughing, and Jasper shook his head.

"I'm glad the whole town is having a laugh at my expense. Wait until you meet him. You'll see."

Kat came from the bar after delivering food to a table of customers and approached the men. "If you three need something to do, I've got plenty of work to go around."

James kissed her on the cheek. "Kat, my dear, we were just taking a moment to tease your son."

Jasper looked at Kat. "I was asking them if I could invite Chris to dinner tomorrow?"

"Santa Claus?"

Jasper raised his hands in the air, then walked out of the restaurant to the sound of James and Beryl laughing. He stopped on the porch and breathed in the moist air. The extended fall weather had left when the rain arrived on Tuesday. Currently, a slight drizzle was falling.

A few minutes later, Kat came through the door.

"I'm sorry, honey. You're such an easy target sometimes. Of course, you can invite Chris. We'd love to have him."

Jasper leaned against the porch railing. "I figured he'd be all alone tomorrow."

She went to him and patted his cheek. "You're very sweet. Please ask him to come."

"I'll ride out there when I'm done here. Jensen's been bugging me to take him to see the reindeer, anyway."

"You can go anytime. Your father and Beryl can finish up."

He kissed her on the cheek. "Thanks, Mom."

Jensen and Micha sat excitedly in the backseat of the Bronco, and Lewis was in the seat next to Jasper. When he heard where Jasper was taking the boys, Lewis had to come along, too.

Jasper glanced at him. "You're going to be cool, right?"

"Yeah. Of course."

When they pulled up to the house, Chris was throwing hay to the reindeer. He stopped when he saw the Bronco and gave a wave.

Lewis stared out the window. "Damn."

Jasper nudged him. "Come on. Close your gaping mouth and get out of the Bronco."

The men helped the two boys out of the backseat, then went to greet Chris, as the boys ran ahead to look through the bars of the pen.

Jasper shook with Chris, then nodded toward Lewis. "This is my brother-in-law, Lewis Jensen."

Chris shook with him. "Nice to meet you, Lewis."

Jasper motioned toward the boys. "And your remember my son, Jensen. And the other one is Micha, Lewis' son."

"Fine looking boys, and I bet they've been good all year."

Lewis raised an eyebrow and Jasper nodded a silent message. *I know. I told you.*

Chris tossed the rest of the hay in the pen, then looked at Jasper. "What brings you out, Chief? Are you checking up on me and the boys?"

"I guess. And Jensen's been bugging me to bring him out here to see the rest of...the boys. I also wanted to invite you to Thanksgiving dinner tomorrow. It's a big gathering. Mostly family, but you're welcome to join us."

"That's very kind of you."

"I thought you'd be here alone, and might want to come in and meet some folks."

"I appreciate the offer. I'd like that very much."

Jasper glanced at Lewis. "Great. We eat at three. We'll start gathering around two. It's at The Sailor's Loft."

"Your mother's restaurant."

"Yes. That's right."

"I haven't gotten into town much. But I drove by it. It's a nice place."

"Yeah. A town staple. Been there since the seventies."

Chris thought for a moment. "And before that, it was a saloon and dance hall, I believe."

"Um...yeah. A while before that. Back in the thirties."

Chris laughed. "I've done a bit of research on your island. Fascinating place."

Lewis finally spoke up. "Are you thinking about sticking around?"

Chris laughed again. "Oh no. Afraid I can't stay. Lots of work to do."

Jasper glanced at Lewis again. "What, ah...kind of work do you do, if I may ask?"

"Manufacturing and sales. A bit of travel. It keeps me busy."

Jasper wanted to ask him who takes care of his reindeer when he's traveling. But he was afraid Chris would tell him they're his transportation.

The boys giggled, and the men turned to see Jensen and Micha standing on the first rail of the pen, petting a reindeer over the top of the fence.

Jasper went to them. "Hey, boys. Get down."

Chris came up behind Jasper. "That's Buck. He's harmless."

"Well, still. It's a little too close." He lifted the boys down off the fence and Buck stuck his nose through as far as his antlers would allow.

"He likes us, Dad."

"You can pet him through the fence. Stay on the ground. And steer clear of his mouth."

"He won't bite us."

"Just do as I say."

"Yes, sir."

"Yes, Uncle Jasper."

Jasper turned back to Chris. "So, we'll see you tomorrow, then?"

"I'll be there. Can I bring anything?"

"Oh no. Just yourself. There will be enough food to feed the whole town."

Lewis came to the fence and tentatively petted Buck's nose.

Micha looked at him. "Isn't he cool, Dad?"

"Yeah. He's super cool." Buck nodded his head and snorted.

After a few more minutes, Jasper and Lewis rounded up the boys and put them into the Bronco, then said goodbye to Chris, who once more promised he'd be there for Thanksgiving dinner.

Jasper drove to the main road while the boys chatted in the back seat about the reindeer. Lewis was quiet until they hit Lighthouse Road. Then he whispered under his breath. "Holy shit."

"Don't say it."

"But..."

Jasper shook his head. "It's not possible."

"But the way he looks. His laugh." He glanced in the backseat at the boys, then mumbled, "Like a bowl full of jelly."

"Lewis."

"Right. Impossible. I know." He was quiet again until they reached Harper's Fork. Then he turned toward Jasper. "Manufacturing and sales? A little travel? Like one night a year?"

Jasper started laughing. "Maybe everyone will make fun of you now, instead of me."

"No. See. I'm going to keep it to myself. You went and blabbed it to everyone."

"The only person I told was your sister. She's the one who told everyone."

"Well, that was your first mistake."

Jasper dropped Lewis and Micha off, then went home. When he got there, his father's truck was in the driveway. James didn't often visit, so him being there was odd.

Jensen leaned forward in his seat. "Is Grandpa here?"

"Looks like it."

They went into the house and found James sitting at the kitchen table with Poppie. He had Gracie in his lap. Seeing his father holding a baby was still strange to him. Even after five years.

"Hey, Dad. Is something going on?"

Poppie took Gracie from James, then poured Jasper a cup of coffee before smiling at Jensen. "I want to hear all about the reindeer." She took his hand and led him to the living room.

Jasper sat at the table. "What's going on?"

"I wanted to give you a weather update."

"A weather update? You could've just called me."

"I also wanted to apologize for teasing you about this Chris character. I know your curiosity is based on your concern for the town."

"It's fine, Dad. I'm a big boy."

"Well, still."

"So, what's with the weather? More rain? That's hardly news."

"Snow, actually."

"Snow? Seriously?"

"Yeah. Seriously."

The island got snow about every twenty years. And even then it was more frozen rain than actual snow and it never accumulated.

"Like actual snow?"

James nodded. "A blizzard warning for tonight."

Jasper laughed. "Are you still messing with me?"

"No. I swear." He took a folded piece of paper from his pocket. "Quinn brought this by before he left town."

Jasper read the report from the National Weather Service. "A blizzard. Go figure. I need to go back to town and let everyone know."

"I contacted the volunteer fire department. They're out there now spreading the word."

James had been chief for years. He knew how to take care of business. "Thanks."

James stood. "So, just stay here and stay warm."

"Is this going to mess up dinner tomorrow?"

"I doubt it. I don't care what the NWS says, snow on Gracie Island isn't going to amount to much."

Chapter Six

"Did we have a little pre-dinner cocktail?"

Poppie was at the French doors, peering out into the dark night.

"Honey, come to bed."

"I want to see the snow. I miss the snow."

"Even if it started snowing right now, you wouldn't be able to see it. It'll either be there in the morning, or it won't."

She left the window and got into bed next to Jasper. She laid down, and he put his arm around her. "You got snow every year in Boston?"

"Yes. Lots of it. Which was a pain to try to get anywhere. But here, it'll just be beautiful."

Jasper kissed the top of her head. "Don't hold out for too much. I was in high school the last time it snowed. And calling it snow was a bit of a stretch. It was more like really cold rain. The temperature dropped below freezing, which it never does, and we had ice in the tide pools."

"How did the meteorologist not see this coming?"

"When they use the words freak snowstorm, it means they're just as surprised as we are."

"Well, I hope for the kids' sake there's at least enough to turn the ground white."

Jasper patted her shoulder. "That'd be cool."

She sat up. "Why aren't you more excited about this?"

"If it actually snows, that just means the calls will start coming in. People stuck in their driveways, accidents on the slippery road. We don't even have a snow plow, so we have no way to clear the roads if it comes to that. Snow means I'll miss Thanksgiving dinner."

She laid back down. "Well, we don't want that. Thanksgiving is your second favorite holiday."

"Next to...?"

"The Fourth of July."

"Christmas is moving up the list since we have kids to share it with."

"Do you not have wonderful Christmas memories from your childhood?"

"Of course. Mom always made it special. My dad would even show up once in a while."

She kissed his neck. "It's only going to get better. This year we have three kids to share it with."

"Gracie doesn't really count yet."

"Maybe. But Tucker will be totally into it."

Jasper laughed. "That kid. How can he and Jensen be so different?"

"Well, from stories I've heard my parents tell, he got it from his Uncle Lewis."

"That makes sense."

When Jasper felt the bed move, he opened his eyes and watched Poppie go to the French doors.

"Well?"

She turned around with a frown. "Not even a dusting."

"I told you not to get your hopes up."

She returned to the bed and sat next to Jasper. "I'm glad we didn't tell the kids. They'd just be disappointed."

"I'll run into the station this morning and check the weather forecast. I suppose it could still come." He patted Poppie's knee. "It can snow all it wants tomorrow. Today, I'm looking forward to turkey."

She smiled. "You're right. We don't want anything to interfere with today." She bent down and kissed him, then got off the bed. "I need to go feed the gang now, so they're hungry later."

"It seems to me they're always hungry."

"That's true. Do you want some eggs this morning?"

"No. I want to be hungry later, too. Is there any of Mom's banana nut bread left?"

"I'll warm you up a couple of slices."

Jasper rolled onto his side and tried to get comfortable again. He was glad it didn't snow. It would've been a novelty for sure. But like he'd told Poppie, it would've caused problems. Especially if there was more than a few inches. He'd never driven the Bronco in snow. But he assumed it could handle five or six inches before it started being a problem. He was pretty sure he'd never have to worry about that.

When Jasper got to the office and checked the weather report, the storm had disappeared. They used the word, dissipated. But Jasper figured that was code word for they didn't know what the hell happened to it. In any case, he was glad the snow never materialized. It was bound to cause havoc on the island, no matter how little there might be.

He left the station and headed for The Sailor's Loft. He stopped for a moment and straightened the sign above the bell.

Twilight and evening bell
And after that the dark!
And may there be no sadness of farewell.
When I embark.

He kissed the ends of his fingers, then touched the sign. "Happy heavenly Thanksgiving, Ivy." He rang the bell three times, then went inside.

As soon as he opened the door, he smelled the turkeys cooking. That, along with fresh baked bread, made his mouth water. He went to the kitchen and found Kat and Peg hard at work.

"Do you need a turkey taster? I'm here to volunteer."

Kat waved at him. "You need to wait like everyone else."

"How about a slice of bread?"

Peg and Kat both said, "No!" at the same time.

"How about some help, then?"

Kat went to him and hugged him. "The best thing you can do for us is to leave us to it."

"Right. I'll see you guys in two hours. Love you Mom."

"I love you more."

He turned back and smiled at Peg. "You too."

"I know. Go on. Get out of here."

Jasper left the kitchen and went to check the bar. The beer cooler was full. The ice was topped off. Apparently, there was nothing for him to do.

He poured himself a Thanksgiving shot of bourbon and drank it down. Then left the restaurant.

When he got home, Poppie was sitting in the kitchen with Tucker and Jensen. Tucker was scribbling on a piece of paper, while Jensen was dictating his Christmas list to Poppie.

"What's going on here?"

"Jensen believes it's time to get his list made."

Jasper kissed Tucker's head, and he looked up and smiled. "Color."

"It's great, Tuck."

Poppie finished the list, then Jensen held it up to Jasper. "Dad, do you want to read it?"

Jasper took the list and read the items. "This is quite the ambitious list."

Jensen shrugged. "I know I won't get it all. I just want to give Santa options."

Jasper handed the list back. "Good call."

Poppie stood and hugged Jasper, then gave him a kiss. She pulled back a few inches and looked at him. "Did we have a little pre-dinner cocktail?"

"It's Thanksgiving. And it was one shot."

She kissed him again. "I kind of like it."

"Well, I'm planning on having a few more with dinner, so good."

They both heard Gracie crying, and when Poppie started to go to her, Jasper stopped her. "I'll get her. I think that's an 'I want my daddy' cry."

He went to Gracie's crib and lifted her up. "Hey there, little miss. What's all this?" Gracie continued to cry and Jasper brought her out to Poppie. "I was wrong. It's an 'I'm hungry' cry."

Poppie took her, and Gracie stopped crying. She smiled at Jasper. "Hmm. Seems she likes her mother."

"That's because you've got the goods."

Jensen called from the table. "Dad?"

"Yes, honey."

Jensen held up a drawing of Santa in his sleigh. "Does this look like Santa?"

Jasper took the drawing from him and studied it for a moment. "That is a perfect rendition of Santa. The reindeer are excellent."

Jensen nodded. "I know. That's because I've seen them in person."

Jasper handed the drawing back. "Yes, you've seen real reindeer."

"Real Santa's reindeer. They're special, Dad. They're not like plain old reindeer. They can fly."

"You should bring that and give it to Grandma. She'll love it." Jasper headed for the front door. "I'll walk the dogs again before we go. I might hike down a way to tire them out."

Poppie smiled. "When are we leaving?"

"An hour or so."

"When you come back in, you can help me get these guys dressed. Jensen and I searched high and low for Tucker's boot. We can't find it anywhere."

"Can't he wear his tennis shoes?"

Tucker looked up at Jasper. "Boot."

"Right. We'll find the boot."

The search for the boot was a success, and the Goodspeed family headed into town for Thanksgiving dinner. When they arrived, Lewis and Sarah were there with Micha, Matty, and Alice. The room was filling up with relatives, and Jasper tried to greet them all.

When Poppie came to him and handed him Gracie, she smiled at him. "I'm going to go see if your mom needs help in the kitchen."

"Don't do it."

She patted his arm. "It'll be fine."

When Jasper spotted Chris coming through the door with a plastic container in his hands, he went to greet him.

Chris shook his hand, then smiled at the baby. "Hello there, Gracie."

Jasper tried to remember if Chris had even seen Gracie, let alone been introduced to her.

Gracie, who was usually shy, smiled at Chris and cooed. Chris laughed. "Aren't you a little angel?"

Jasper looked around the room. "Most everyone is here. Go introduce yourself if you want. Most of them won't bite."

Chris laughed. "I'll do that." He wandered off and Lewis came up to Jasper.

"How'd that go?"

"He knew Gracie's name."

Lewis watched Chris make the rounds. Everyone was welcoming and treated him like part of the family. "The guy is either some sort of mind reader…"

"Or?"

"Or he's Santa Claus."

Jasper patted Lewis' shoulder. "Come on. Let's go get some eggnog."

They headed for the bar, and Lewis glanced at Gracie. "Is she allowed in here?"

"This girl spent her first nine months behind the bar. She was inside her mother, but still."

"She's an old pro, then."

"That's what I figure."

Jasper went behind the bar and took a pitcher of eggnog from the refrigerator. As he was adding rum to two glasses, Poppie came up to the bar.

"Why is my daughter behind the bar?"

"She's helping me serve eggnog to her uncle."

"Hmm." She reached across the bar and took Gracie from Jasper. "Will you pour me one without the rum, please?"

"Of course."

As Jasper filled another glass, Chris came into the bar. "What's going on in here?"

"Having some eggnog. Can I pour you a glass?"

"Sure. I love eggnog."

Jasper held up the bottle of rum. "Rum?"

"Of course. It isn't eggnog without rum." He patted Poppie's back. "Unless you have a good excuse not to add it."

Jasper handed the drink to Chris, and he held it up for a toast. "Christmas cheer to one and all."

They all tapped glasses and took a drink, then Chris said, "I appreciate you inviting me, Chief."

"Of course. I'm glad you came."

Chris set his drink on the bar and took a folded piece of paper from his pocket. "Young Jensen gave this to me." He held up Jensen's Christmas list.

"Man, sorry about that."

Chris laughed his laugh. "No problem." He tucked it back in his pocket. "I'll see to it that it gets into the right hands." He picked up his drink and headed for the dining room.

Jasper poured himself a shot of rum and drank it down. "He's friggin' Santa Claus."

Chapter Seven

"I think the Chief Deputy is a bit tipsy."

When dinner was announced, they went to the dining room and took their places at the table. Lewis and Jasper sat next to each other, with Sarah and Poppie sitting next to their husbands with the children divided up and sitting with their corresponding cousin. All of the Jensen kids were just a few months older than the Goodspeed children. So Jensen and Micha were best buddies. As were Tucker and Matty. Matty didn't seem at all bothered by Tucker's regression to one-word communication. The girls were still too young to hang out. But there was no doubt they would in time.

Lewis returned to his seat after filling a plate with food. He sat and nudged Jasper.

"So, how are we going to prove this?"

"We're not. I'm going to leave it alone."

"Bull. It's killing you not knowing."

"Despite what I said a few minutes ago, obviously, the man is just a man." He picked up a piece of bread and dipped it into his gravy.

"Okay. Whatever makes you comfortable."

"Just eat your turkey."

Jasper never drank when he was on duty, which, technically, he was today. But he'd also never had a call come through on Thanksgiving Day. Even so, he should've stopped after the eggnog and the shot of rum. He shouldn't have had a beer with dinner. But he did.

Poppie smiled at him. "I think the Chief Deputy is a bit tipsy."

"Nah. I'm good."

"Okay."

He scowled at her, then smiled. "Everyone is home eating turkey. No one is looking to cause trouble."

"I hope so. I'd hate to see your sterling reputation tarnished."

He glanced at Chris, who was having an animated conversation with the mayor. Thomas Steele was Maisy's husband and Jasper's second cousin. He was a direct descendant of Henry and Alma.

Poppie glanced at the two men, then nudged Jasper. "You'll know soon enough."

"How so?"

"If he disappears on Christmas Eve."

Jasper's scowl returned. "He's not Santa Claus."

As always happens on Thanksgiving, everyone ate too much. So after dinner, it was time to work off some calories. Jasper, Lewis, and Sarah went onto the stage in the bar and prepared to play some music. They'd been playing together for almost ten years and they specialized in the old sea shanties passed down for generations. It was fun and lively music and the audience always got into it. Tonight they'd be especially appreciative since most of them had been drinking more than Jasper had.

Throwing caution to the wind, Jasper brought a second beer up on stage with him. It was late. It seemed he'd made it through the day without a call.

The band started playing and the family members joined in on the singing. After an hour, Jasper needed to rest his voice.

He addressed the crowd. "Hey, I need to take a thirty. But we'll be back. Get yourselves another drink. Or some of Mom's pumpkin pie."

Kat called out. "There's cheesecake, and pecan pie, too. And someone brought some lovely Christmas cookies."

Jasper stepped off the stage and went to Poppie and the kids. Gracie was asleep in Poppie's arms.

"How is she sleeping through the music?"

"She's used to it. She hears it every Friday night."

Jasper kissed Gracie's cheek, then Poppie's forehead. "I'm going to get some pie. Can I bring you a piece?"

"Yes please. Can I have a little slice of each?"

"Coming right up."

Jasper went to the table with several pies, three cheese cakes, and a plate of amazing Christmas cookies. He looked at Kat, who was slicing the cheese cake into serving-sized pieces.

"Who brought these?"

She shrugged. "I don't know. But they're almost too pretty to eat."

The cookies were shaped like Christmas trees, bells, snowmen, and reindeer. They were all intricately iced with amazing detail.

Jasper picked one up. "*Almost* too pretty to eat." He took a bite. He'd grown up eating his mother's pastries. They were wonderful. But there was something about the cookie he couldn't explain. "Have you tried these?"

"No."

He broke off a piece and handed it to her. "Try it."

Kat ate the bite, then raised her eyebrows. "Tastes like—"

"Christmas?" Jasper turned to see Chris standing next to him. "It took me years to perfect the recipe."

"You made these?"

"Yes. What do you think?"

"It's the perfect Christmas cookie."

Chris held his stomach and laughed. "Thank you. That's what I was going for."

"You made these in Sam's kitchen? I've seen the kitchen. It's not set up to make something like this."

"It's the ingredients that count. Not the oven they were baked in."

"Well, they're amazing. I need to take one to Poppie and the kids."

"That's why I brought them."

Jasper took a slice of pecan pie and a slice of pumpkin pie, along with three cookies, then he glanced at Chris.

"How'd you like the music?"

"Love it. I don't suppose you'd let an old man join in on a few songs with you?"

"Sure. We've got a tambourine with no one to play it."

"Perfect."

"Join us on the stage in twenty minutes."

Jasper returned to Poppie and set his bounty on the table, then sat next to her.

She picked up a cookie. "Aren't these beautiful. Who made them?" Jasper cocked his head. "No way."

He nodded. "Take a bite."

Poppie took a bite, then looked at Jasper.

"Right? What's it taste like?"

"Christmas."

"He says it's taken him years to perfect the recipe."

"Like millennia?"

Jasper shrugged. "I don't know."

Poppie nodded. "Mr. Smith, I don't know where you came from, but wherever it is, you make a darn good cookie."

They shared the two pieces of pie and tracked down the boys who were playing with their cousins to give them a cookie. Then it was time for Jasper to go back on stage with Lewis and Sarah.

Jasper went to the mic. "We're going to have someone join us for a few songs. Chris. You ready to come up?"

Chris made his way through the group to the sound of cheering. Chris had made an impression on everyone and seemed to be welcomed into the family. He came onto the stage and Sarah handed him the tambourine.

He smiled at Jasper. "Just play, I'll catch on."

"Okay. Here we go."

They started playing and Chris jumped right in, following the beat with the tambourine. On the second song, he joined Jasper on the chorus. He had a great voice, and it complimented Jasper's perfectly.

At the end of the song, Jasper addressed the audience. "How about that? The man can sing."

Everyone clapped and cheered, then Jasper waited for them to quiet down before starting the next song. It was a slow melancholy song and when Chris came in with some harmonies, the audience went silent. Jasper couldn't believe how good Chris was.

When the song was over, Jasper put a hand on Chris' shoulder. "Man, anytime you want to join us, you're welcome to."

Chris laughed. "Thank you, Chief. I appreciate it. I don't mean to overstep, but isn't it about time for some Christmas carols?"

Jasper nodded. "I believe you're right." He turned to Sarah. "Let's dust off some Christmas tunes."

They spent the next hour playing Christmas music and Chris stayed on stage the whole time. By the time the set was over, it was getting late, at least for the kids in the crowd. And Jasper announced they were calling it a night.

"Take your time leaving. But Mom and Peg have been here since daybreak. They need to go home."

As everyone started preparing to leave, Jasper returned to Poppie's table. Maisy was sitting with her with Alice asleep on her lap.

"What did you think, Maisy?"

"I think you should offer him a place in the band."

"I did." Jasper sat down as Sarah came to the table and took Alice from Maisy.

"Thank you Maisy."

"Of course. You know I love holding babies."

Jasper looked around the room. "Speaking of babies. Where are my sons? And my nephews?"

Maisy smiled. "Last I saw them, James, Thomas, and Beryl were entertaining them."

"By doing what?"

"I don't know. But all seven of them were laughing."

Lewis came up to the table with two beers in his hand. He held one out to Jasper. "One for the road?"

Jasper looked at Poppie and she smiled. "Go ahead. I'll drive home."

He grinned. "I love having a wife who doesn't drink."

"It's not that I don't drink. I've been pregnant or nursing for the last six years. You've just forgotten and so have I."

He took a sip of his beer and sat next to her. "As soon as Gracie is weaned, will play another game of Questions. If I can find a couple cans of that grapefruit crap."

"By then, I'll just drink the gin straight. But I don't think I can think up any more questions. I think I know everything there is to know about you."

"Hmm. We'll see. I think I still have a secret or two."

Maisy patted her hand. "Give it a few months and enjoy, before you're expecting the next one."

Poppie shook her head. "Oh no. I think we're done."

Maisy winked at Jasper. "Isn't that what she said after Tucker?"

"Yep."

Poppie shook her head. "That was before I had Gracie in a jail cell while a hurricane was raging outside."

Maisy laughed. "I guess that's a pretty good reason to call it quits."

The restaurant was emptying out and Jasper and Lewis were finishing up their beers. The boys had joined them and were eating another cookie.

Jasper looked at Tucker. "What do you think? Good cookie?"

Tucker looked at what was left of his snowman shaped cookie. "Santa."

Jasper sighed, then straightened in his chair when the phone rang. He watched James go to answer it. When James glanced in this direction, Jasper set down his beer.

Maisy laughed. "I guess that's a pretty good reason to call it quits."

The restaurant was emptying out and Jasper and Lewis were finishing up their beers. The boys had joined them and were eating another cookie.

Jasper looked at Tucker. "What do you think? Good cookie?"

Tucker looked at what was left of his snowman shaped cookie. "Santa."

Jasper sighed, then straightened in his chair when the phone rang. He watched James go to answer it. When James glanced in this direction, Jasper set down his beer.

"Shit."

James hung up the phone and crossed the room to Jasper. "That was Betty Sweeton."

"What's wrong?"

"She says there's a reindeer in her front yard."

Chapter Eight

"Oh my. Santa has a girlfriend."

Betty lived near Harper's Fork in the house she'd lived in all her life. She was close to seventy, but she was sharp as ever. If she said there was a reindeer in her yard, then there was a reindeer in her yard.

Jasper called for Chris, who was talking with Kat, and he crossed the room to the table.

"Is everything okay, Chief?"

"I think one of your reindeer got out."

"Did someone see him?"

"Yeah. A woman who lives near the fork. About five miles from your place. He's in her yard. Apparently not in any hurry to leave."

"Well, I'll be. It must be Buck. I guess I'd better go round him up."

Jasper stood. "I'll come with you."

James sighed. "I'll drive."

Jasper looked at his half-finished third beer. "Right." He looked at Poppie. "Can you get home okay?"

"Yes, my love. It's not even nine o'clock. We'll be fine."

He kissed her, then pointed at the boys. "Be good and go to bed when you get home. It's past your bedtime."

Jensen nodded and gave him a salute. "Yes, sir, Chief."

Tucker watched Jensen, then saluted too, "Chief."

Jasper grinned. "Thank you, junior deputies."

James, Jasper, and Chris headed for the door, but Jasper veered off at the last minute to go say goodnight to Kat and Peg.

He hugged them both. "Thank you for all of this. It was great, as always."

"Of course, sweetheart. Be safe out there."

"It's a reindeer, Mom. I'll be fine."

"I'll see you tomorrow. Come in for lunch. We've got lots of leftover turkey."

"I'll see you tomorrow for lunch. Love you."

"I love you more."

He joined Chris and James at the door and they went outside to a light rain. James looked at Chris. "Do you want to follow us in your vehicle?"

"Yes. I'll be right behind you."

Jasper watched Chris walk to an old pickup and get inside.

James put a hand on his shoulder. "Come on, son. We're getting wet."

"I have a feeling we're going to get a lot wetter before we get this runaway reindeer back where he belongs."

They got into James' truck and headed out of town toward Harper's Fork. They continued straight for a quarter of a mile, then pulled into Betty's driveway. She came onto her porch when she heard them drive up.

James and Jasper got out of the truck and met her on the porch.

"Evening Chief and ex-Chief."

James nodded. "Betty. Where did you see this reindeer?"

"I swear I really saw him."

He smiled. "We believe you."

Chris arrived, and when he came onto the porch, James turned to him. "This is Chris Smith. The reindeer belongs to him."

Betty smiled at Chris. "My goodness. How interesting."

Chris chuckled. "Hope he didn't frighten you, ma'am. He's harmless."

"I'm sure he is. He's just so big."

Jasper cleared his throat. "Um. Betty. Where did you see him?"

"He was right out my kitchen window eating what's left of my garden. Not much to eat in there, I'm afraid."

"Around the side of the house, then?"

"Yes." She pointed to the left side of her house. "Right over there. Do you want me to show you?"

James smiled at her. "No. You stay here where it's dry. We'll go track him down."

The men headed around the left side of the house with two flashlights and went through the open gate of the large garden space. The reindeer was near the back, eating a forgotten pumpkin.

James closed the gate and Chris approached the reindeer. "Buck. What are you doing?"

Buck snorted, then continued eating the pumpkin.

Chris moved closer to him. "Come on now, time to go home." He whistled, then after one last bite, Buck left the pumpkin and walked over to Chris. "That's a good boy." He attached a rope to Buck's halter and rubbed his ears.

James was staring at the reindeer and Jasper put a hand on his back. "Now you see why I've been having some trouble with all of this?"

James nodded. "For the first time in five years, I'm sorry I'm retired. I'd love to see how this all turns out."

"I'd be glad to reinstate you. Just until Christmas, of course."

Chris approached them, leading Buck. "I can tie him to the back of the truck and lead him home. This isn't the first time he's taken off. As you well know."

James nodded, still not quite believing what he was seeing. "We'll follow you to make sure you make it back safe."

"I'd appreciate it."

They walked to the front of the house and Betty was on the porch. "Oh my. Isn't he something?"

Chris laughed. "Would you like to pet him? He's harmless."

"Can I?"

"Sure. Come on down." Chris handed the rope to Jasper and went to take Betty's arm as she came down the steps. "Watch your step, there."

Jasper looked at James and raised an eyebrow as Betty tentatively touched Buck.

Chris laughed. "Give him a good pet."

Betty stroked Buck's neck, then glanced at Chris. "He's magnificent."

"That he is."

Jasper was about tired of standing in the rain holding a reindeer while Chris showed him off to Betty. He cleared his throat. "Probably should get him back. Don't you think?"

Chris looked at him and nodded. "Sure." He took Betty's arm and walked her back up the steps. "You have a good night, Betty."

"Oh. You too."

James waved. "Good night, Betty."

"Good night Chief." She looked at Jasper. "Chief."

Chris tied the rope to a metal ring attached to the tailgate of the truck, then got in behind the wheel. "I'll take it slow."

James nodded. "We'll stay back a way so we don't spook him."

Chris started driving and James pulled in behind him, keeping the reindeer in the headlights, but staying far enough away to not make him feel rushed.

James glanced at Jasper. "You saw a reindeer once when you were a kid. Do you remember that?"

"No." He didn't remember doing anything with his father as a kid.

"Your mother and I took you to the mainland to see Santa. You must've been Jensen's age or there about. He had a reindeer with him. It was a scraggly thing. Nothing like that guy."

Jasper glanced at him. "It's weird, right? That he's here on the island. Chris and all of his reindeer. A month before Christmas."

"Yes, son. It's very weird. He should be at the north pole getting ready for Christmas Eve."

Jasper leaned back in the seat and didn't respond.

They arrived at the house without incident and while Chris untied Buck, Jasper and James went to look at the pen. The wooden rail fence was still there. But inside of it was a new wire fence with a gate, which was securely closed and latched. There didn't appear to be any breaks in the fence line. And with those antlers, he certainly didn't go under it.

James looked at the other seven reindeer. "Damn strange."

Chris approached the gate and opened it, then released Buck. "There you go, boy."

He closed the gate and smiled at Jasper. "Thanks for the backup. I think we're all good now."

"When did you put up the wire fence?"

"Got it done the other day. The wooden rails weren't really sufficient to keep in my boys."

Jasper wanted to mention the wire fence didn't seem to be doing the trick, either. But he didn't. "How do you suppose he got out? The gate was latched."

"Buck's a tricky one. He's quite a jumper."

Jasper raised an eyebrow. The fence was six-feet high.

James came up to him. "You might have to put a lid on the pen to keep them in."

Chris laughed. "Just might have to do that." He shook hands with both men. "Thanks again."

Jasper and James headed for the truck and drove away from the house. Jasper looked back to see Chris waving.

"There's no way a reindeer that big could've gotten enough distance and speed to clear the fence from inside of it."

James nodded. "The damn thing had to have flown over it. There's no other explanation." Jasper turned in his seat toward James, who started laughing. "I'm kidding, Jasper. Obviously, we don't know what reindeer are capable of."

Jasper didn't truly believe Buck had flown out of the pen. But he also didn't think it was possible for him to jump the fence, either. There had to be a reasonable explanation. And the only one he could think of that didn't defy the laws of gravity was that someone let him out. But who would do that? He sighed and James looked at him.

"Go home and get some sleep, son. You're not going to solve this mystery tonight."

James dropped him in front of his house and Jasper waved from the porch before going inside. Poppie was sitting on the couch with a book.

Jasper took off his wet jacket and removed his soaked boots before going to sit on the table in front of the couch.

Poppie set her book aside and patted his knee. "You're really wet. How'd it go?"

"Buck is safely tucked into the pen. But I don't know for how long."

"Was the gate left open?"

"No. And the wooden pen you saw the other day has been replaced by a six-foot wire one. So, I'm thinking Chris anticipated his boys getting over the wooden one."

"Can a reindeer jump that high?"

"It seems unlikely without a running start. The pen is twenty feet at most."

"So, what are you thinking?"

He frowned at her. "I'm trying not to think about it too much. At least not tonight."

She patted his knee again. "How was Betty?"

"Betty was fine. She thought Buck was a magnificent creature."

"I agree with that."

"She also seemed to think Chris was pretty…interesting as well."

"Interesting how?"

"There was definitely some blushing involved."

"Oh my. Santa has a girlfriend."

Jasper stood and stretched. "I need to go take a hot shower."

"Want some company?"

"You have to ask?"

"Let me check on the kids and grab the baby monitor."

Chapter Nine

"Well, they are Santa's reindeer."

Poppie parked in front of the clinic and looked at Gracie and Tucker in the backseat. Tucker was running a fever and would want to be carried, which would be tough with Gracie in tow, too. But she could do it. It wouldn't be the first time she hauled two kids around at the same time. She released Gracie's car seat and set it on the sidewalk, then got Tucker out of his seat. He clung to her and laid his warm cheek against her neck.

Poppie rubbed his back. "Okay, sweetheart. Dr. Hannigan will make you feel all better real soon."

As she closed the car door, Chris came up to her. "Can I give you a hand?"

"If you could get us inside, that'd be great."

He put a hand on Tucker's back. "Feeling under the weather, son?"

Tucker snuggled deeper into Poppie's neck, and Chris lifted Gracie's carseat, then opened the clinic door. Poppie went through it and Amy came out from behind the counter to greet her.

"What's going on with Mr. Tucker here?"

"He's got a fever that I can't bring down."

"Have a seat, and I'll take you to a room in a few minutes."

"Thank you, Amy."

She went to a row of chairs and sat down with Tucker on her lap. Chris put Gracie's seat down, then sat next to Poppie. "I'll stay until you get called back."

"Thank you."

Tucker looked at Chris, then held his arms out to him. Poppie smiled. "I don't think he's contagious. But you don't need to take him."

"Nonsense. If you don't mind."

Poppie handed Tucker to Chris, and he laid his head on Chris' shoulder and patted his chest. "Santa."

Poppie shook her head. "I'm sorry. He has this idea—"

He chuckled. "Don't worry about it. I get that a lot."

"Will you be staying on the island, Chris? I think everyone has taken to you."

"I'd love to. This place is special. But I'll be moving along soon."

"Too rainy for you? The weather takes some getting used to."

Christ thought for a moment. "The rain's fine. It's a lot milder than my weather back home."

"Snow?"

"Yeah. Lots of it."

"Jasper said you're from up north?" *With a vague reference to Canada.*

"That's right."

Poppie didn't want to push for details, even though she was dying to. "Well, we'll miss you."

"I'll miss you folks, too. But I'll pop in from time to time."

Like every December twenty-fourth?

Amy came over to them. "The doctor is ready for you now." Amy picked up Gracie's car seat and Poppie took Tucker from Chris. "Thanks for your help."

"My pleasure. Hope Tucker feels better soon."

Poppie followed Amy to an examination room and Amy glanced over her shoulder at Chris. "Is it just me? Or does he look exactly like—"

"It's not just you."

Jasper crossed the street and went down a couple of blocks to the clinic. He'd been on a call, but Maisy told him Poppie had called and was at the clinic with Tucker. As he went through the clinic door, Chris was coming out.

"Whoa. Sorry." Jasper stepped back and held the door for Chris. "Are you ill, Chris?"

"No. I was helping Poppie with the kids. They just went back to a room."

"Oh. Well, thanks."

"No problem. I'll let you get in to them." He headed down the street and Jasper went inside.

Amy smiled at him. "They're in room two."

"Thanks, Amy."

He went down the hall to room two and went inside. When Tucker saw him, he held his arms out. Jasper took him from Poppie.

"What's going on here, buddy?" He looked at Poppie.

"He spiked a fever. Probably his ears again."

"Well, it is that time of year."

A few minutes later, Dr. Hannigan came in and confirmed Poppie's suspicions.

"You know the drill. You've been through this the last two years. Tylenol to get his fever down and I'll mix you up an antibiotic. It'll be ready in about an hour."

Jasper shook with the doctor. "Thanks, Doc. I'll be back for it in a while."

Dr. Hannigan left, and Poppie smiled at Jasper. "I could've called it in."

He smiled. "Yeah. But then you wouldn't have spent time with Chris."

She shook her head. "Tucker called him Santa."

Jasper laughed. "Oh my gosh. What did Chris say?"

"He said he gets it a lot. He also said he gets a lot of snow back home. And he said he'd be leaving soon, but would pop in from time to time."

"Like every Christmas Eve?"

She laughed. "Whoever or whatever Chris is, he's a very nice man."

"I agree."

They left the clinic and Jasper helped Poppie put the kids into the car. "I'll go get the Bronco and follow you home."

"I'm fine, honey."

"I know. But there's nothing going on, and I'd like to get you home and get Tucker settled in."

"Thank you. I welcome the help and the company."

"I'll be right behind you."

Jasper walked to the station to get the Bronco, then caught up to Poppie, and followed her home. When she pulled up short in the drive, he stopped behind her and got out of the Bronco. All eight of Chris' reindeer were in the yard in front of the house.

He went to Poppie's window and when she rolled it down, he said, "Well, shit."

Poppie laughed. "So, do you suppose they all jumped over the six-foot fence?"

He opened her door. "Come on. Let's get you three inside. Then I'll deal with our visitors."

He took Tucker from the backseat and Poppie got Gracie. They skirted around the reindeer, who paid them no mind, and went inside.

Jasper laid Tucker on the couch and covered him with his favorite blanket. Poppie put sleeping Gracie in her crib, then joined Jasper, who was looking through the window at the reindeer.

"So, how are you going to handle that, Chief?"

Jasper sighed. "First, I'm going to call for backup." He went to the phone and dialed the station.

"Sheriff's office."

"Hey, Maisy. I need you to put out a call for some help at my place."

"What's going on? Is everyone okay?"

"We're fine. We just have eight antlered visitors."

"Oh, my."

"Yeah. See if you can track down Lance and at least one other guy."

"Sure thing, sweetheart."

Jasper hung up the phone and rubbed his chin. "I learned a lot of things at the police academy. But nothing about rounding up reindeer."

Poppie patted his back. "You'll figure out something. You always do."

He nodded and went out to the porch. After a few minutes, Lewis drove up.

He smiled at the reindeer before joining Jasper on the porch. Jasper looked at him. "I didn't know you were on the official sheriff's posse list."

"I'm not. I heard it on the scanner." He scowled. "Why aren't I on the list? I've help you out a lot over the last thirteen years."

Jasper shrugged. "I can put you on the list."

"Would I get paid?"

"No. It's a voluntary position. Like the fire department."

"Oh. Then never mind. I'd rather voluntarily help you on my own time."

Lance pulled up a few minutes later with Mellie.

Lewis nudged Jasper. "Mellie's on the list?"

"Nope. She just likes to keep an eye on Lance."

Mellie got out of the truck and looked at the reindeer. "I heard about these guys, but...wow."

She and Lance joined Jasper and Lewis on the porch. Lance studied the reindeer for a moment. "When you told me the old guy had reindeer, I didn't really think about them being *reindeer*!" He turned to Jasper. "What's the plan?"

"The other day Chris led Buck back by tying him to the back of his vehicles. But we can't tie all eight of them. Even with three trucks."

Mellie put her hands on her hips. "What if we tie one to each of our vehicles? The others will probably follow."

Jasper shrugged. "Let's give it a go. I'll get some rope." He got three lengths of rope, then since no one was volunteering, he went to Star and tied an end to his halter. He then led Star to the Bronco and tied him to it.

He knew Buck was gentle. He wasn't sure about the rest of them. But Star had cooperated. He tried to remember which ones were Regi and Rex. He was pretty sure they were the ones with the shorter antlers.

He walked slowly up to one of them, and the reindeer let him tie the rope to his halter. While he was doing that, the other came up to his buddy. Jasper put a line on him, then tied one to Lewis' truck and one to Lance's.

"These two guys like to stay close to each other. So I'll lead and you two drive side-by-side if you can. With any luck, the other five will follow us."

Jasper went to his truck and made a wide, slow turn to head down the driveway. Lance did the same, followed by Lewis. The reindeer cooperated and didn't fight the lead. They headed down the drive at a couple miles per hour, and after a moment, the other reindeer followed their friends. At a snail's pace, they drove toward Chris' place.

When Jasper pulled into Chris' driveway, his truck wasn't there. Jasper got out of the Bronco as Lewis and Lance pulled in next to him. As before, the gate was secured.

Mellie and Lance came up next to Jasper as he was checking the pen. Lance scratched at his short beard. "So how the hell did they get out of there?"

Mellie looked at the top of the fencing and grinned. "Well, they are Santa's reindeer."

Jasper shook his head. "They didn't fly out."

"Okay. Whatever you say."

"I looked it up the other day. They can jump really high. Higher than this fence."

"Without a running start?"

"It would seem so."

"Hmm. I like the idea of flying better."

At a sound of a vehicle coming up the road, they all turned to see Chris pull up. He took in his reindeer outside of the pen and the three tied to the trucks.

Jasper went to him as he got out of his truck. "We found them in front of my house."

"Oh, dear. Thank you for bringing them back."

"I don't think they like being contained."

"You could be right." He went to the gate and opened it, then got some hay from a small shed. "They're not animals that like to be confined." He put the hay in the pen while Jasper untied the three reindeer. All eight of them went into the pen to eat the hay.

"I'm sure the folks around here won't mind them wandering around. I just wouldn't want to see them get hurt. Hit by a car or something."

"I'll try to keep them in the pen, but it seems it may not work. But don't worry, we won't be here much longer."

"Okay, Chris. If they get out again, we'll bring them back."

"Thank you." He looked at the others. "Thanks for helping the Chief bring them back."

Lewis nodded. "Sure. No problem."

Mellie went to Chris and introduced herself. "I'm Mellie. I own the Rusty Pelican."

"Nice to meet you, Mellie. You have a son."

"Yes, I do."

"I hear he's a good boy."

"He is, thank you."

Jasper cleared his throat. "I should get back to town. I'm out of range out here."

Chris looked at him. "That must be inconvenient for you."

"Yeah. We lose the radio a mile or so past the fork."

"What would it take to fix that?"

"Money. We'd need to extend the tower on top of the station. But with our weather, it'd have to be solid. Someday, the town will have the money to put one up."

"Okay. Well, thanks again."

"Have a good night, Chris."

Mellie walked with Jasper to the Bronco, then glanced at Chris, who was still at the pen. "Did you tell him I had a son?"

"No. I've never even mentioned you to him. The guy has mysterious powers."

"Because he's Santa?"

"No. Because he just wants to mess with me."

"I'm sure that's not true."

"Well, intentional or not, Chris Smith has been messing with me since he got here."

Chapter Ten

"And the reindeer take the outfield."

The Sharks and the Barracudas had been rivals for as long as Jasper could remember. The two baseball teams played each other every Sunday nine months out of the year. The last game of the year was always on the Sunday after Thanksgiving. There had only been a handful of times when the weather was too bad for them to play. But they always managed to make it up before Christmas.

Today it wasn't raining but the cloud cover assured it would be soon. Hopefully, it'd hold off until after the game. But it didn't really matter. They'd keep playing as long as they could see the ball.

Jasper got to the park a little early to set up the bases and clear debris from the infield. When he spotted Lewis, he tossed an armload of twigs and leaves into the garbage barrel and gave him a smile.

"Are you ready to kick some ass today?" The Sharks had won the last ten final games of the year. Mostly due to Lewis' pitching.

"Yeah. About that." He took his right hand out of his coat pocket. It had a bandage wrapped around it.

"What the hell happened?"

"Sliced it at work yesterday."

"Why didn't you tell me sooner?"

"I didn't want you to worry about it. And I was hoping it'd be better today. At least well enough to pitch." He smiled at Jasper. "You can pitch."

"Yeah. But then who will play first? I'm much better on first."

"Mark?"

"Mark is barely adequate."

"Well, today, he's better than me."

When Chris came walking across the field, Jasper and Lewis both looked at him.

Jasper smiled. "How you doing, Chris?"

"What's going on here? I heard something about a ballgame."

"Yeah. Sharks versus Barracudas. It's tradition."

"I love baseball." He looked at Lewis. "What's troubling you, son?"

Lewis held up his hand. "I'm the pitcher."

"Oh my. Do you have a backup pitcher?"

"Jasper. But we really need him on first."

"Hmm. I'm not sure how this all works, but if you're open to a temporary player, I've pitched a ball or two in my day."

Jasper knew there was something special about Chris. Maybe not magical. But some sort of extraordinary powers. So if Chris said he could pitch, Jasper was inclined to believe him. He went to a canvas bag and took out two gloves and a ball.

"Let's see what you got."

Chris chuckled as he slid his hand into the glove and punched it a couple of times. He tossed the ball a few times in the air to get the feel for it, as Jasper backed up twenty feet.

Chris looked at him. "It might take me a couple to warm up."

"Take your time."

The first ball was a bit tentative, but it went right to Jasper. He tossed it back to Chris.

"Put a little heat on it this time, Chris."

Chris wound up and pitched the ball. It came fast and right on target. Jasper tossed it back, then backed up a few more feet.

Lewis laughed. "Holy shit. You've got an arm, Chris."

Chris took a moment, then threw another perfect ball.

Jasper grinned. "That's good enough for me. Lewis, find this man a blue shirt."

They headed for the backstop and James met them by home plate. "What's going on here?"

James was the pitcher for the Barracudas. He was good. But not as good as Lewis. The fact Lewis was thirty or so years younger also helped.

"Lewis hurt his hand and can't pitch. Chris here is filling in. I assume that's okay with you."

James nodded. "Sure." Jasper could see his father anticipating their first win in ten years. "Fine by me."

James wandered off and Jasper put his hand on Chris' shoulder. "He thinks he's got it in the bag."

Chris laughed. "He might have to work for it a little."

"I'd prefer he goes home with another loss."

Chris nodded. "I'll do my best." He looked at Jasper. "Why aren't you two on the same team?"

"It's a family thing. My mom's family were all Sharks. The Goodspeeds have always been Barracudas. I could go either way. I chose Sharks."

"So, who does your mother cheer for?"

"She's very diplomatic. She cheers for both sides."

The stands started filling up as the players from both teams started arriving. Most of the Sharks were surprised by their stand-in pitcher. But they all knew how important upholding their winning streak was to Jasper. If Chris proved himself to Jasper, that was good enough for everyone else. They all welcomed him to the team and Lewis brought him a Shark's t-shirt and a ball cap. Chris tucked his green wool cap into his back pocket and put on the cap.

Lewis grinned. "There you go. You're one of us now."

Jasper spotted Poppie and the kids in the stands sitting with Sarah and her kids. He waved and Poppie threw him a kiss. The boys both stood up and saluted, and Jasper saluted back. Then he returned his attention to his team and the game.

The Sharks were the first to take the field, and the crowd cheered when Chris stepped onto the pitcher's mound. He tipped the hat Lewis had given him, then took a moment to prepare himself.

James was first up at bat, and Jasper watched closely. His father was a good pitcher and a decent batter. And right now, Jasper was sure James was feeling pretty confident.

The first ball was a little wild and James let it go. Chris collected himself, then threw the second one into the strike zone. James swung, and the ball flew past the short stop. As James ran for first, the centerfielder caught the ball on a bounce and threw it to Jasper.

James made it safe to first a few seconds before Jasper caught the ball.

"Nice one, Chief." Jasper grinned. "Do you need a minute to catch your breath? We can call a time out. Get you a chair."

"Just throw the damn ball in."

Jasper threw the ball to Chris. "What do you think of our pitcher?"

"I think you found another ringer."

"I swear he just walked onto the field and volunteered. I had no idea he could pitch."

"Hmm. I think he's been pitching up in the North Pole for a while."

Jasper laughed. "You could be right."

The next player struck out. And the second one hit a fly ball to center field that was caught making the third out. James never got beyond first.

Chris wasn't as good as Lewis, but he was good enough. The Sharks took home their eleventh win in a row. Following the yearly tradition, everyone went to The Sailor's Loft after the game. Chris was the man of the hour, at least to the Shark's fans. Though quite a few Barracuda fans congratulated him, too.

Jasper invited Chris to sit at the table with the family. He sat between Jensen and Tucker, while Jasper and Poppie, with Gracie, sat across from them.

"Hell of a game, Chris."

"It was great fun. Thanks for letting me play. I'll get your shirt back to you."

"No. You keep it. You earned it."

Jensen tapped Chris' arm. "Do they play baseball at the North Pole?"

Chris laughed. "I imagine they do. Only I expect they use snowballs instead of baseballs. And icicles for bats."

Jensen laughed. "You're funny."

Jasper grinned, "And the reindeer take the outfield."

Jensen cocked his head. "Reindeer don't have hands, Dad. They can't catch the ball."

"Oh. Right. Must be elves then." Apparently, he wasn't nearly as funny as Chris.

Poppie smiled. "Well, I'm impressed, Chris. Not only did you pitch a winning game, but you almost got a home run."

"Almost doesn't count in baseball, Poppie."

"Well, impressive none the less."

Peg brought a platter of hamburgers to the table. "Does this work for you, Chris?"

"Sure. Baseball and hamburgers. Can't beat it."

During dinner Jensen wanted to know all about the reindeer, so Chris spent the meal giving Jensen as much information as he felt a child could understand. Jensen hung on every word and no doubt would share it all with Micha the first chance he got.

The rain had started while they were inside the restaurant, and it began pouring on the drive home. When they arrived at the house, Jasper pulled as close as he could to the porch, then he picked both boys up and carried them inside before coming back out to help Poppie with Gracie. When he got inside, he started a fire in the fireplace.

The big rock fireplace was the only thing left after Jasper's house burned down seven years ago. He and his grandfather had built it. And when it came time to clear away the debris from the fire, he wanted to preserve it. The new house was built around it.

He was pretty wet, but he'd just need to take the dogs out soon for a walk, so there was no sense in changing. He stood by the fire, as he often did, to dry out.

Jensen came over and stood next to him. "Dad?"

"Yes, honey."

"Was Chris kidding about the icicle bats and snowballs?"

"Yes. I imagine it's pretty hard to play baseball at the North Pole. You'd lose the ball in the snow after the first hit."

"Then how come Chris is so good at playing baseball?"

Jasper turned to face the fire and held his hands near the heat. "He says he's played before. I don't know where or when. But he's a pretty good pitcher."

"He's not as good as Uncle Lewis, though."

"No. Uncle Lewis is the best."

Jensen was quiet for a few moments, then said, "Dad?"

"Yes?"

"When I grow up can I play with you on the Sharks team?"

"Of course. What position do you want to play?"

He thought about it for a moment. "I think catcher."

"Why catcher?"

Jensen shrugged. "I don't know. It just seems fun."

"Well, that's a pretty good reason to do it then."

Jensen looked up at Jasper. "Will you teach me how to catch?"

"Of course. We'll work on that this summer."

"Cool."

"Dad?"

"Yes, Jensen."

"Do still not believe Chris is really Santa Claus?"

Jasper needed to take a moment to answer. "I truly don't know."

Jensen took his hand. "I knew he'd wear you down."

Chapter Eleven

"Do sharks celebrate Christmas?"

There hadn't been anymore reindeer sightings and Jasper hadn't seen Chris since the baseball game. He'd resolved to stop trying to figure it all out. It was almost Christmas. Things had been slower than normal around town, and he'd just be thankful for that.

Jensen was spending the afternoon at the station while Poppie worked her afternoon shift at the bar. Sarah always watched Tucker and Gracie. But Jasper took Jensen when he could to give her a bit of a break and bring the number of kids down from six to five. On the two afternoons Poppie worked, he was usually able to keep him. Even if it meant leaving him with Maisy if Jasper got a quick call in town.

Jensen was sitting in front of Jasper's desk with a coloring book. He'd just finished filling in the outline of a shark with a green crayon. He held it up to show Jasper.

"What do you think, Dad?"

"It's a green shark. Very nice."

"He's a Christmas shark."

"Oh, okay."

"Do sharks celebrate Christmas?"

"Um…I don't see why not."

"Cool. I'm going to make his friend red."

"Good call." Jasper leaned back in his chair and stretched. "How about some lunch, Junior Deputy?"

"Yes, please."

"Chicken strips from the deli?"

Jensen nodded. "My favorite."

"Okay. Put your things away. Mom will be off soon and will be taking you home."

"Are you coming home, too?"

"Not yet. I've got some more work to do in the office."

Jasper helped Jensen into his coat, then put on his own before leaving the office. Maisy looked up from her counter.

"Where are you two men off to?"

Jensen yelled out, "Chicken strips."

"Mmm. Sounds good."

Jasper opened the front door. "I'll be on the radio or at the Loft."

"Okay, sweetheart."

They went outside into the brisk December weather. It wasn't raining. But it was December, so it would be soon.

"Dad?"

"Yes, honey."

"Why does Maisy call you sweetheart?"

Jasper smiled. "The same reason she calls you sweetheart. Because she loves us."

Jensen frowned. "But she's not grandma or Aunt Peg."

"I've known Maisy all my life. She's like a mom to me. Which makes her like a grandma to you."

Jensen seemed satisfied with his father's answer and he skipped ahead on the wooden sidewalk. When they were across the street from the grocery store, Jasper caught up to him and put a hand on Jensen's shoulder to stop him from crossing the street.

"Hold up." Chris and Betty were sitting outside at one of the picnic tables. They seemed to be deep in conversation and didn't see Jasper and Jensen across the street. "Let's go eat at the Loft instead."

"But I want chicken strips."

"Grandma can make you some chicken strips. Come on." Jasper knew if he went to say hi to Chris, all the weirdness would return. It was interesting he was having lunch with Betty, though. Chris moved fast. Probably because he'll be gone in a few weeks. Jasper shook his head. *Don't go there again.*

They continued down the street to the loft, then crossed the street and stopped at the mast.

"Can I ring it, Dad?"

"Go ahead."

Jensen rang the bell three times, then they went inside. Jasper had explained why they rang the bell every time they passed it, a few months ago. And Jensen seemed to grasp the concept of loss and honoring those they loved. At least as well as a five-year-old could.

Peg delivered some food to a table, then came to greet them. "Are you here to eat?"

Jensen looked up at her. "Can Grandma make chicken strips?"

"Of course she can. Do you want to come into the kitchen and help her make them?"

"Yeah."

Peg looked at Jasper. "What can I get you?"

Jasper thought for a moment. "A burger. Fries. I'll be in with Poppie."

"Okay. I'll bring it into you." She took Jensen's hand. "Come on, young man. Before you know it, you'll be cooking in the kitchen right alongside your grandmother."

Jasper went into the bar, which was empty. He took a stool and smiled at Poppie. "Busy day?"

"I had a few customers. I might go home early, though, if Peg's okay with handling the bar until Mark comes in."

"I'm pretty sure she won't have a problem with that."

"Are you here to see me? Or to eat?"

"Both."

"Where's our son?"

"I thought he was with you."

Poppie slapped his arm. "Stop. I hate it when you do that."

"No you don't. You don't ever hate me. You love me too much."

"You're right. I do. Did you get extra food so I can have some too?"

"Um...sure. I'm always thinking about you and whether or not you're hungry. I only wanted a half of a burger."

She shook her head. "I'm going to go order my own burger."

"I'll go."

"No. It's fine. I want to say hi to Jensen, anyway." She came around the bar and kissed him before heading for the kitchen.

Jasper watched her go, then went around the bar and poured himself a coke. He smiled when he saw Lance walk up to the bar.

"Doesn't the county pay you enough, Chief? Are you in here moonlighting to make a little extra Christmas money?"

"Just holding down the fort for Poppie. Why are you slumming here? Did Mellie finally come to her senses and eighty-six you from the Rusty Pelican?"

"I came to see Poppie, actually."

"What do you want with my wife?"

Lance grinned. "I have a message for her. A secret Christmas message."

"Hmm. Likely story."

Poppie came back through the door and smiled at Lance. "Hey. What are you doing here?"

He took her arm and pulled her further away from the bar, then whispered into her ear.

She smiled and nodded, then patted his arm. Lance looked at Jasper and gave him a wave.

"See you later, Chief."

"Bye, Lance."

Poppie came up to the bar and took a seat on a stool. "What are you drinking?"

"What was that all about?"

"Nothing."

"Nothing my ass."

"It's a secret. Will you pour me a Coke, please?"

"What kind of secret?"

"Jasper, what time of year is it?"

He sighed. "Christmas."

She nodded and picked up his Coke.

He poured another, then leaned on the bar. "But we aren't exchanging gifts this year. So we shouldn't have any secrets."

"I decided I didn't like that plan. It was a stupid plan we made in June. Who makes Christmas related plans in June?"

He took a sip of the Coke. "So you got me a present?"

"Possibly." She studied him for a moment. "You didn't stick to the plan, did you?"

"Of course I did. We agreed." He went around the bar and sat next to her.

She put her arm around his shoulders. "You're lying to me."

"I'd never."

"What did you get me?"

"Poppie. I swear I didn't get you anything."

She removed her arm and took another drink, then she looked at him through the mirror and started laughing. "You're a big fat liar."

He turned to her and grinned. "I guess you'll find out Christmas morning if that's true. Now. Are you ready for some gossip?"

"Always."

"Guess who was sitting in front of the grocery store having lunch together?"

She thought for a moment. "No clue. It's freezing. Why would someone eat outside?"

He scowled. "Jensen and I were going to. But I didn't want to interrupt...Chris and Betty."

"Aww. That's so cute. Are they dating?"

Jasper shrugged. "I guess you could call it that."

"Adorable."

"Yeah. I wonder if she knows he'll be gone for Christmas."

"So, if he's Santa—"

"Don't start."

Peg came in with two burgers and set the plates on the bar in front of them. "Enjoy."

Poppie smiled. "Thanks, Peg. Is Jensen behaving?"

"Always. He loves helping in the kitchen."

Jasper picked up his burger. "I might be the last Goodspeed in the sheriff's office."

"Why do you say that?"

"Maybe Jensen won't want to follow in his father's footsteps. Maybe he wants to be a chef instead of a chief."

"Just because he likes helping in the kitchen doesn't mean he won't want to be a deputy like his father. He loves hanging out with you at the office."

"Hmm."

"And what about Tucker?"

Jasper shook his head. "You can't have a criminal record."

Poppie nudged him. "Stop denigrating our youngest son. Tucker is not going to grow up to be a criminal."

"I'll still love him."

Poppie sighed. "Ridiculous. And there's Gracie, too. Maybe she'll be Gracie Island's first female chief."

"Hmm. I could get behind that."

"So there's hope. One of the children will carry on the Goodspeed family legacy and be the fifth generation upholding the law on Gracie Island."

"I hope so. But of course, they're going to do what they're going to do. I won't stand in their way. Unless Tucker takes a wrong turn somewhere along the line. Then I might intervene."

Poppie shook her head. "Poor Tucker. He's a little bulldog. But he's a sweet bulldog."

"Yes, he is. I just hope he starts talking again one of these days."

She patted his hand. "I promise you he will."

Jasper turned and looked at her. "So what did you get me?"

"I'm not telling you what I got, any more than you're going to tell me."

"Actually, I am going to tell you."

She smiled. "Really?"

"Yes. I made you a list."

"A list?"

"The ten things I love about you."

She set her burger down. "That's sweet, but I don't believe you."

He shrugged. "Whatever."

"If that's true, then give me one. One reason off the list. Number one."

"They're not in any particular order."

"Just one."

He thought for a moment. "I love how...gullible you are."

She pushed him and he nearly went off the stool. She laughed and grabbed his arm as he put a foot down to catch himself. "Whoops. I'm sorry. But you totally deserved that."

"I almost dropped my burger."

She took a sip of Coke. "So, if you were actually going to make a list. What would be on it?"

"Just one thing?"

"Sure."

"I love what a good mother you are."

"Aww. That's sweet."

He shrugged. "I can be sweet."

"Do you want to know one thing from my hypothetical list?"

"Sure."

"I love how sexy you are."

"Wow. Shallow."

She laughed. "I don't care. It's the truth. You're just as sexy today as you were the day I met you."

"Drunk at the Rusty Pelican?"

"No. A couple of days after that."

"That was only seven years ago. I would hope I've still got a few sexy years ahead of me."

"Oh you do. Forty is going to look really good on you."

"Hey. Not so fast."

She whispered in his ear. "You just turned thirty-seven."

"Hush."

She kissed his neck, then resumed eating.

"I've got another one for you."

She smiled. "Tell me."

"I love how you can't keep a secret."

"I can keep a secret."

He shook his head. "I'll bet you a back rub, you won't make it to Christmas without telling me what you got me."

"You're on, mister. I'll even up the bet and throw in a foot massage. Can you handle that?"

"Deal." He stuck out his hand, and she shook it.

She resumed eating. "I wonder if Betty knows Chris has a wife waiting for him at the North Pole?"

Chapter Twelve

"You just need to believe, Chief."

Jasper was at his desk when Maisy came to the door. "Betty Sweeton just called. The reindeer is back."

Jasper leaned back in his chair. "Of course it is."

"Do you want me to send Quinn? He's about finished at the pier."

"No, I'll go. Unfortunately, I'm now an experienced transporter of runaway reindeer."

"Okay."

Jasper took his jacket from the rack by the door and headed out of the office. He was feeling a little cooped up. It'd be nice to get outside for a while. He got into the Bronco and drove to Betty's house.

Buck was standing in front of the house and Betty was tossing him something from the safety of the porch. She stopped and waved when Jasper got out of the vehicle.

"Afternoon, Chief."

"Betty. He's back, huh?"

"Yes. And he loves my cornbread muffins."

"We all do, Betty." She always brought them to the monthly game night potluck.

Jasper took a rope from the back of the Bronco and approached Buck from the side so he could see him coming and wouldn't startle. Buck eyed Jasper, then continued chewing his muffin.

"Toss him one more."

She did and Jasper hooked the rope to Buck's collar when he bent down to grab the muffin.

"Okay, Buck. Let's go home."

Betty waved. "Say hi to Chris for me."

"Will do. Have a good day."

He tied Buck to the back of the Bronco and gave him a pet. "I'm getting tired of hauling your ass down Lighthouse Road."

Buck tossed his head and snorted as Jasper got into the truck.

He pulled away from Betty's and drove slowly down the road, taking the turn onto Lighthouse Road. It had rained earlier in the day and more rain was expected soon. The road was muddy and a bit slippery. But Jasper had been driving these roads since he was sixteen. It'd take a lot more than a little mud to throw him.

When he pulled in front of the house, Chris was on the porch. He had a cup in his hand and he waved it at Jasper.

Jasper stopped the Bronco and got out. "Found Buck at Betty's again. Seems he's partial to her cornbread muffins."

Chris laughed. "I'm sure he is." He stood, then grabbed the porch support to steady himself.

Jasper looked at him. "Are you okay, Chris?"

"Sure. Fine. Would you mind putting Buck in the pen?"

"No problem. I got it." Jasper untied Buck, then took him to the pen and released him inside. He rolled the rope up and tossed it into the back of the Bronco before going onto the porch. Upon closer inspection, Chris appeared to be drunk.

"Have you been drinking, Chris?"

He looked shocked by the question. "Drinking? No. I don't drink. Other than an eggnog now and then."

"What's in the cup?"

"Cider." He picked up a ceramic jug. "Found it in the cellar."

Jasper took the jug from Chris and smelled it, then grinned. "This cider has gone hard."

Chris squinted at him. "Hard? Do you mean it's bad?"

"No. I'm guessing it's pretty good. But it's fermented. You're drunk, Chris."

He looked astounded for a moment, then started laughing. "No wonder it tastes so good."

"Would you care to have a sip, Chief?"

"I'm on duty."

"Can you sit a spell, then?"

Jasper shook his head. "No. I need to get back. I don't want to be out of range too long."

"Right, the radio signal stops at the fork."

"There about, yeah."

Chris thought for a moment. "Maybe there's something I can do about that."

"I appreciate that, Chris. But like I said, the other day, it's going to cost a lot of money to extend the tower and improve the range."

Chris pointed at him. "You just need to believe, Chief."

"I'm not sure believing will work in this case."

"You never know."

"Okay. Well, I need to get back. You might want to lay off the cider."

Chris laughed again. "Will do, Chief."

"And don't drive anywhere for a while."

"I'll stay put."

"Okay. You have a good night, Chris."

"You too, Chief."

As Jasper headed back for town, the rain started. By the time he got to the station, it was pouring. He parked right out front and dashed inside. Maisy came from behind the counter to help him with his wet coat. She took it from him and hung it by the door.

Jasper ran his hands through his wet hair. "Is Quinn back?"

"He was. But then Mellie called about some trouble at the Pelican."

"Do I need to go over there?"

"Quinn said he'd call if he needed backup."

"Okay. Lance is probably there, too. He spends most of his time there with Mellie whether he's working or not."

Maisy shook her head. "When are those two going to get married?"

"I don't know. I think they're pretty happy with things the way they are."

"I suppose so. Let me get you some coffee."

Jasper went to the counter to wait for his coffee, then went to his office. Not much was going to happen with the rain. But he'd stay until five. He thought about Chris drinking the hard cider.

"Santa Claus was wasted."

Jasper looked through the messages on his desk. Maisy had a habit of writing each phone message on post-it notes. They were color coordinated to represent the level of importance. She'd stick them to the corner of his desk, arranged by color.

There were four messages that came in while he was gone. None of them were written on yellow, which was Maisy's choice for urgent. But one caught Jasper's attention. It was from Evan Jeffers. Jasper had sent him an email the day after he'd met Chris. At the time, he was still wary of Chris and why he was there. He wasn't concerned anymore, and he'd just let it go. But Evan had finally gotten back to him.

He picked up the phone and dialed the number.

"Hello?"

"Evan? This is Chief Goodspeed."

"Oh. Hey. Sorry it took me so long to get back to you."

"No problem."

"You say there's someone living on my dad's property?"

Jasper's heart sank a little. "Yeah. Were you not aware of it?"

"No. No one contacted me about staying there. And frankly, I don't see why anyone would want to. Is he still there?"

"Yeah. Older man. Nice as can be. He's not here to cause trouble. Says he's going to be gone by Christmas."

Evan was quiet for a few moments. "Hmm. Well, honestly, I don't really care. Especially if he's leaving soon. What's he doing out there? The place is barely inhabitable."

Jasper sighed. "He's... I don't know exactly."

"Well, would you mind keeping an eye on him? And if he's not gone by Christmas, then we'll reassess the situation."

"Sure thing."

"Thank you, Chief."

"You're welcome. I'll call you back after Christmas."

"Happy holidays."

"Same to you." Jasper hung up the phone and leaned back in his chair. "Why'd you lie to me, Chris?"

The rain lasted for three more days, and on the fourth, Jasper got to the office early. The fog had lifted, and it was a rare, partly-sunny December day. When he pulled up to the station, there was a truck parked in his spot. He parked behind it and got out. He didn't see anyone around and he was about to go in and ask Maisy if she knew who the truck belong to, when he heard a noise on top of the building.

He walked to the middle of the street and looked up at the roof. There were two men working.

"Hey! What are you doing up there?"

Jasper couldn't hear the men's reply. He was about to ask again when a car honked and he moved to the side of the road. The car belonged to Mayor Steele.

"Good morning, Chief. I was hoping to beat you here."

"What's going on?"

"Come inside. I'll tell you all about it."

Thomas parked his car and the two men went into the office. Maisy came out to greet her husband, then she glanced at the ceiling. "What's going on up there?"

"Can you get me some coffee, honey?"

"Sure."

She poured two cups and handed one to Thomas and one to Jasper. "Why are those men on our roof?"

Thomas smiled. "Great news. Wonderful news."

Jasper was getting as impatient as Maisy. "What news, Thomas?"

"You're getting your radio tower, Jasper."

"What?"

"It'll be done by tomorrow if this weather holds."

"How?"

"An anonymous donor. Someone paid for the whole thing. And told the men to get it up as soon as possible."

"An anonymous donor? Who would do that?"

Thomas laughed. "I don't know. That's why it's anonymous."

Maisy clasped her hands. "Oh my goodness. What a gift."

Jasper still needed answers. "I don't understand."

Thomas patted him on the shoulder. "The only thing you need to understand is that you'll soon have radio reception on most of the island. Maybe not all the way to the lighthouse. But certainly past the fork."

Jasper remembered the coffee in his hand and took a sip. "I need to go talk to someone."

Thomas laughed. "Jasper, this is great news. It's not a mystery for you to solve."

Jasper handed his cup to Maisy. "I'll be back in a while. Call Quinn if something comes up."

"Sure thing, sweetheart."

Jasper drove to the fork and turned onto Lighthouse Road. He'd decided not to question Chris about why he lied to him about contacting Evan. He instinctively trusted Chris and wanted to just let things play out. If Chris was still there after Christmas, then maybe he'd confront him. For now he'd wait and see. But now, this anonymous donor situation had him wondering again about who Chris was and why he was there. He drove to Sam Jeffer's house and found Chris throwing hay to the reindeer.

"Good morning, Chief. What brings you out here? All the boys are accounted for."

"Someone donated the money to have the radio tower extended."

Chris smiled. "That's great news." He tossed the last of the hay and turned to Jasper. "Isn't it?"

"Yes, of course." He took a moment before asking the question he needed to ask. "Was it you, Chris?"

Chris put a hand to his chest. "Me? Where would I get that kind of money? I'm basically squatting on a dead man's property." Did he just admit that Evan had no idea he was there?

"But you're the only one I've talked to about it."

"I'm sure everyone in town knows your radio is limited."

"No one in town has that kind of money, either. If they did, we would've had it a lot sooner."

Chris took his arm. "Come sit on the porch. Let me get you some coffee. I know it's early, but I have some Christmas cookies, too."

Jasper let Chris take him to the porch, then sat down while Chris went in to get the coffee. He returned a few minutes later with two cups and a plate with more beautiful Christmas cookies on it. He set it on a table between the two chairs, then handed Jasper a cup of coffee.

He sat and took a sip from his cup. "It's a Christmas miracle, Jasper. Just accept it and be thankful."

Jasper drank some coffee and picked up a Christmas cookie. He glanced at Chris. "I'm sorry I came charging out here."

"It's no problem."

"I just..."

"Chief, you've got to believe that sometimes good things happen. You don't need to look for the why or the how. Just accept the gift and be thankful."

Jasper thought for a moment, then got to his feet. "I need to go, Chris."

"Don't rush off."

"I've got to go talk to someone." He held up the cookie. "Thanks for the cookie and the coffee." He took another sip of coffee then set the cup down. "I'll see you, Chris."

"Have a good day, Chief."

Jasper drove straight home and went inside. Poppie was in the living room with the kids and was surprised to see him.

"Is everything okay?"

"Yes." He went to her and gave her a hug and a kiss.

"Jasper, why are you home in the middle of the morning?"

"Come out to the porch with me." She glanced at the kids and he took her hand. "They'll be fine for a moment."

She nodded and went with him to the porch. "What's going on, Jasper?"

"I was just out talking to Chris. I thought he did something. But it wasn't him. It couldn't have been him. But that's all beside the point. He said something that made me realize I've never thanked you."

"Thanked me? For what?"

He put his hands on her waist and pulled her in close. "For this." He glanced at the house. "For all of this."

"Jasper, what we have, we built together."

"But you saved me, Poppie. You blew into my life and pulled me out of a two-year depression. You showed me it was okay to be happy again. To love again. To believe good things could happen."

She put her arms around his neck. "Well, if you insist on thanking me. You're welcome. But honestly, I think we taught each other how to be happy. How to love joyously and unconditionally. You gave me this house and those three kids inside. You gave me a life on Gracie Island."

He smiled. "Okay. We'll call it a tie."

Poppie laughed. "I love you Jasper."

"I love you too, Penelope."

Chapter Thirteen

"That was an interesting night."

Christmas was only a couple of weeks away, and Jensen had been begging Jasper to get a tree. But getting a tree wasn't an easy task on Gracie Island. It was against the law to cut down a tree on the island. Not that there were many to begin with. And none would make for the perfect Christmas tree. So getting a tree meant going to the mainland and hauling it back on the ferry. It was fine, and Jasper did it every year. This year, for some reason, he was dragging his feet. But he was determined to go over the weekend. The kids deserved to have a Christmas tree to enjoy well before Christmas. He'd stalled long enough.

It'd been an annoying day with a lot of small complaints keeping both him and Quinn busy. Nothing too crazy. Just the typical small-town mischief that seemed to escalate around the holidays. But it was Friday and Jasper would be off tomorrow. The perfect time to make the trip to the mainland for the tree. He'd make his weekly run out Lighthouse Road, then take Jensen on the ferry to the mainland.

At five o'clock, Jasper left the office and headed home. When he pulled up to the house, he was surprised to see a Christmas tree sitting on the porch.

"What the hell?"

He got out of the Bronco and went onto the porch. The tree was freshly cut and a beautifully shaped fir with silvery green foliage. It was a perfect tree.

Jasper went inside the house and found Poppie in the kitchen making dinner. Gracie was in her playpen, gurgling and babbling to herself.

When Poppie heard Jasper come in, she gave him a smile. "Oh, hey honey." She looked at him closely. "You look tired."

"Long day. Where did the tree come from?"

"Tree?"

"There's a Christmas tree on our porch."

Poppie washed her hands, then picked Gracie up and headed for the front door. When she saw the tree, she smiled at Jasper, who had followed her outside. "You went to the mainland and got us a tree today? I thought you were going tomorrow."

"I didn't get it. It was here when I came home. You didn't hear someone dropping off a tree?"

"No. Are you teasing me?"

"No. I swear. Call Maisy, she'll tell you I was on back-to-back calls all day."

She touched the branches. "Maybe Lewis dropped it off. Or James. I don't know why they wouldn't come in and say hi, though."

Jasper raised his hands. "You know what? I'm not going to question it. Whoever left it for us will either claim responsibility or they won't." He open the door and called the boys. "Come out here for a second, guys."

The boys ran out and squealed when they saw the tree.

Jensen jumped up and down. "Can we decorate it tonight, Dad? Please?"

Jasper laughed. "Of course we can. It's a big tree. It's going to take a couple of strong men to get it inside. Do you want to help me?"

"Yeah." Jensen bent his arms and flexed his non-existent muscles.

Jasper did the same, and Poppie put a hand on his bicep. "As impressive as this is. Let's put them away for now."

Jasper laughed. "I'll bring them out later."

Poppie kissed him, then took Tucker and Gracie inside. She kept Tucker occupied while Jasper and Jensen brought the tree in the house and set it up in front of the big window. At night, the lights would be visible from the driveway. It took them a while to get it straight and secured in the tree stand. With Tucker running around this year, Jasper wanted to be extra cautious.

He stood back to make sure the tree was straight one final time. "Looks good, Junior Deputy."

"Can we put the decorations on it?"

"After dinner. We'll put the lights on, then we'll decorate it."

"Cool!"

Poppie came out of the kitchen with Gracie and Tucker. Tucker stopped walking when he saw the tree.

He pointed. "Uh oh."

Jasper laughed and picked him up. "Why uh oh?"

"Tree."

It's a Christmas tree. We're going to hang pretty things on it and put presents under it."

Tucker clapped his hands. "Santa?"

"Yes, honey, Santa."

Jensen tugged on Tucker's foot. "Santa *Claus*."

Tucker nodded. "Santa Claus."

Jasper grinned. "There you go. Santa Claus."

Tucker clapped again. "Santa Claus. Santa Claus."

Jasper looked at Poppie. "Great. Now he's not going to stop saying it."

She laughed. "You wanted him to say more than one word at a time."

After dinner, Jensen helped Jasper with the lights, then the boys hung the ornaments on the bottom half of the tree. Poppie took care of the top half while Jasper was in charge of handing out the ornaments. The last item and the finishing touch was the angel for the top. She was actually a mermaid.

It was the traditional tree topper for most of the Christmas trees on the island. At least all the trees belonging to descendants of Henry and Alma Gracie. It had long since been passed down that for Alma's first Christmas on the island, she insisted Henry find her a mermaid for the top of her tree. If they brought good luck to the sailors, surely they'd bring good luck to Gracie Island. For as long as Jasper could remember, there was a mermaid at the top of the Goodspeed's Christmas trees.

Jasper handed Jensen the mermaid he and Poppie picked out their first Christmas together, then picked him up.

"Okay, son. Put the finishing touch on our tree." Jensen hung the mermaid at the very top of the tree, then Jasper set him down. "Perfect."

Poppie came up beside Jasper and put her arm around him. "It is perfect."

Jasper kissed her. "How about some hot chocolate?"

The boys were in the kitchen with their hot chocolate and Jasper and Poppie were on the couch enjoying the Christmas tree.

Poppie laid her head on Jasper's shoulder. "How does it get prettier every year?"

"I think we just appreciate it more each year. The kids add more and more to the season as they get older."

"And of course, this year Santa Claus is visiting the island."

Jasper laughed. "There is that."

When Sam ran to the door and barked, Jasper went to the window and laughed. "Speak of the devil."

"Who is it?"

"Chris." He went to the door and opened it. "Evening Chris. Is everything okay?"

"Sure. I was visiting Miss Sweeton. I wanted to apologize for Buck's last visit to her place. Then she invited me to dinner, and I got to see why Buck is so fond of her cornbread muffins." He looked at the tree through the window. "I see you got her up?"

"Yeah. You wouldn't happen to know how the perfect Christmas tree ended up on my porch, would you?"

Chris came up the steps. "I figured you were busy, and I have a friend who has a knack for finding perfect trees. Just thought I'd help you and the family out."

"That's really kind of you, Chris. Come on inside."

"I guess I can stay for a minute."

"Long enough for a cup of cocoa?"

"I believe so."

Chris went into the house and nodded at Poppie. "Evening Poppie."

"Chris. Did I just hear you're responsible for leaving this lovely tree on our porch?"

Chris took off his stocking cap and stuck it in his coat pocket. "Yes, ma'am. I figured the kids were itching to have a tree."

"Thank you. It's beautiful." She stood. "I'll go get you some cocoa."

As Chris went to stand by the fireplace. Jensen and Tucker ran into the room. Jensen went to him and hugged him. "Thank you for the tree, Chris."

Chris laughed his infectious laugh. "You're welcome, young man."

Tucker went to Jasper and hid behind his legs. He looked up at his father and whispered, "Santa Claus."

Jasper patted Tucker's head, then sat on the couch. Tucker crawled up next to him as Poppie returned with a cup of hot chocolate for Chris. Jensen went to sit by the tree and Poppie took a chair.

Chris looked around the living room. "This is a nice home you've got here, Chief."

"Thank you."

"I heard you did most of the work yourself."

He shook his head. "No. I had a lot of help. And all the credit for the interior goes to Poppie."

"A collaboration. I like that." Chris took a sip of his cocoa. "Mmm. I love cocoa."

Jasper laughed. "Next to a little hard cider?"

Poppie shook her head. "I believe hard cider is probably the last alcoholic drink I had. Fourth of July, six years ago."

Jasper glanced at Jensen. "That was an interesting night."

Chris laughed. "I imagine hard cider is responsible for a lot of interesting nights."

Jensen laid down with his head under the tree and looked up at the lights. "Chris?"

"Yes, Jensen."

"How come we have Christmas trees?"

"Well, as far as my knowledge goes, it started a long time ago in Germany. The first trees were called Paradise trees, and they represented the Garden of Eden. A few years passed and trees became the symbol of the season with small gifts, cookies, candies, and candles hung from the branches." He walked over to the tree. "Today, most trees represent family traditions with the ornaments holding special memories." He touched an ornament Jasper made in grade school. "Memories passed down from father to son."

"Do you have a Christmas tree, Chris? With your memories on it?"

Chris laughed. "Of course I do. But not here. It's back home."

Jensen sat and looked up at Chris. "I bet you're anxious to get back to it."

Chris patted his head. "That I am, young Jensen. That I am."

Jasper looked at Poppie and raised an eyebrow.

Poppie nodded, then looked at Chris. "If you'd like to join us on Christmas day, you're more than welcome, Chris. We'd love to have you."

"Thank you, Poppie. But the boys and I will be home for Christmas."

Chapter Fourteen

"Not my job, Chief."

On Monday, Jasper made his weekly sweep through the neighborhoods and he noticed most everyone had a tree in the window or lights on the outside of their homes. With the island's severe winter weather, the residents had to be careful about what was used on the outside of the homes. But a lot of people managed to come up with things that worked. Even if it was just a string of lights.

When Jasper drove by Burt's house, he spotted him on his porch tugging on a Christmas tree. Every year, someone made sure he had a small tree. But this was a big one, like the one Chris left on Jasper's porch. A big beautiful Christmas tree.

Jasper pulled over in front of the house and parked the Bronco, then went up to Burt's porch. "Can I give you a hand, Burt?"

"It's a big tree, Chief. A big, big tree. I never had a tree this big before."

"It sure is. Who brought it to you this year?"

Burt shrugged. "Don't know. I found it on my porch. Did you bring it to me, Chief?"

"No, it wasn't me." Burt was trying to pull the tree through the door top end first. "Let's turn this around." Jasper helped Burt turn the tree, then they pulled it into the house. "Do you have a stand? And some decorations?"

Burt nodded. "In the garage. I'll go get them."

"Okay. I'll help you get it set up."

While Burt went to the garage, Jasper used the phone to call the office.

Maisy answered in her bright, happy way. "Good morning, Sheriff's office."

"Morning, Maisy."

"Chief. Are you on your way in?"

"I got waylaid at Burt's house. Whoever supplied his tree this year went all out. It's huge. I'm going to help him get it set up. Then I'll be in."

"No problem. Quinn's here. He and Thomas are setting up a tree in the reception area. Burt's not the only one who had a tree dropped off over the weekend."

"Huh. Okay. I'll be in soon." Someone spent the weekend dropping off Christmas trees. He wondered how many of the trees he saw today were from the mysterious tree donator. It was too big of a job for one man, that being Chris, to pull off. Then again, if he was Santa Claus. Jasper shook his head. *Of course he's not Santa Claus.*

Burt came through the front door loaded down with two boxes with a tree stand balanced on top of them. Jasper took the top box and the tree stand from him and set them on the floor.

"Okay. Where do you want your tree?"

Burt pointed at the front window. "Right there so everyone can see how big it is."

"Okay. Sounds good."

With a little bit of help from Burt, Jasper secured the tree in the stand and moved it to the window. "How's that?"

Burt ran out the front door and stood in the lawn for a moment, then came back inside. "That's perfect, Chief. Can you help with the lights? I want lights so everyone can see it."

"Sure." Jasper took two strings of lights and plugged them into the wall to see if they were working. Neither string came on.

Burt frown. "Oh no. I have to have lights, Chief."

Jasper patted his shoulder. "We'll get you lights, Burt." He went to the phone and called the office again. When Maisy answered, he asked to speak to Quinn.

"What's up, Chief?"

"Can you leave the tree decorating to Thomas and Maisy and run to the mercantile? Burt needs some new lights for his tree."

"Sure. I'll go right now. I'll be there in thirty."

Jasper looked at Burt. "My deputy is going to bring you some lights. He'll be here soon."

Burt smiled. "I get lights on my tree?"

"Yeah. We'll fix you right up." Jasper looked around the house. "Is there anything I can help you with while I'm here?

Burt thought for a moment. "My dishes."

"Your dishes?"

"Yeah. I don't have any clean ones left."

Jasper laughed. "Let's go wash some dishes."

"I don't like washing dishes."

"How about I wash and you dry?"

"Okay, Chief."

By the time Quinn got to the house, Jasper and Burt had cleaned up the kitchen and Burt had clean dishes again.

Quinn helped Jasper string the lights on the tree, and Burt was delighted with how it looked. He hugged Jasper. "Thank you, Chief."

Jasper patted Burt's back. "You're welcome. Can you hang the decorations yourself?"

"Yes, sir."

"Okay. We'll leave you to it, then."

Quinn walked Jasper to the Bronco. "I was in charge of getting Burt's tree this year. I didn't get it yet. And I wouldn't have gotten him such a big one."

Jasper smiled. "Don't worry about it. I think it was an anonymous donor."

"Like the tower?"

"Yeah. Like the tower." Quinn had walked over, so they drove back to the station together. When they went inside, Jasper was surprised that the tree was even bigger than his and Burt's.

"Wow. That's a beauty."

Maisy smiled. "Isn't it though? And Burt and us aren't the only ones blessed with a beautiful tree. We've been getting calls all morning thanking us. Everyone thinks it's the fire department's doing."

Jasper laughed. "I guess we can take the credit."

Maisy cocked her head. "Now, now. Let's give credit where credit's due. This has something to do with our visitor, doesn't it?"

"Chris?"

"Yes."

"Well, he came by Friday night and admitted to leaving a tree on my porch. But half the town? I don't know how he'd pull that off." Jasper thought for a moment. "I'm going to go talk to Jake."

"Don't try to analyze it, sweetheart. Just take the gift and be thankful."

Maisy's words echoing Chris' made Jasper stop for a moment. Then he sighed. "I'll see what Jake has to say. No matter who brought them over, the trees had to come on the ferry."

He left the office and headed for the marina. The ferry would be there for another hour. Jasper found Jake in Duke's office. Duke was the harbor master, and he also kept a pretty close eye on what and who came onto the island.

Duke removed the bottle of bourbon from his desk and smiled at Jasper. "Chief. How're you doing?"

"I just wanted to ask you guys if a truck load of Christmas trees came over from the mainland Friday or Saturday."

Jake nodded. "Yes, sir. It sure did. Early Friday morning. First run."

"Who was driving it?"

Jake shrugged. "Don't know. Didn't recognize them."

"You didn't ask?"

"Not my job. I'd figured you'd know who they were seeing as you're the chief and all."

"Right. Did they leave?"

"The truck is sitting on the ferry."

"Right now?"

"Yeah. Waiting for the next run."

Jasper patted Jake on the shoulder. "Thanks." He left the office and headed for the ferry. When he boarded, he looked around. There were a few locals on board, but most everyone waited until the last minute. When he spotted two men he didn't recognize, he walked over to them.

One of the men turned and smiled at him. "Afternoon officer."

Jasper returned his smile. "Do you two belong to that truck that brought the trees over?"

The man nodded. "Yes, sir. Got them all unloaded, just like we were instructed."

"May I ask who instructed you to bring trees over and distribute them on the island? It's great. And I thank you. I'm just curious."

"Didn't get a name. Or a face, for that matter. Just got written instructions."

"Any chance I can see those instructions?"

The man pulled a piece of paper from his pocket. "Damnedest thing. It's hand written."

Jasper took the list and read it over. In very neat printing were the names and addresses of fifty Gracie Island residents. Most of them were elderly, or in some way not easily able to get a tree themselves.

"Can I keep this?"

The man shrugged. "Sure thing. Jobs over."

"Thank you. And thanks for bringing the trees."

"Just a bit of a Christmas miracle, I guess."

Jasper nodded. "Merry Christmas, gentlemen."

Jasper wanted to believe Chris was behind this. He didn't know how or why. Or if it was even possible. He wanted to let it go, and just take the gift and be thankful. He could do that.

Jasper left the ferry and went down the pier, looking for Lewis. He found him on a private fishing boat sanding down the teak benches.

Lewis looked up at Jasper and smiled. "How goes the mystery of Santa and his reindeer?"

"It's still a mystery. Did you have a tree on your porch this morning?"

"No. Why?"

"You have a tree, right?"

"Yeah. Put it up last week."

Jasper rubbed the back of his neck. "Someone brought a truckload of trees over the weekend and distributed them to everyone without a tree."

"Did you get one?"

"Yeah. So did Burt. And one was dropped off at the station."

Lewis sat on his freshly sanded bench. "So, if I had dragged my feet like you, I could've saved myself seventy bucks?"

"I think you're missing the point. I don't know where the trees came from."

"Do you think our visitor had something to do with it?"

"No. How could he?" Lewis raised an eyebrow and Jasper scowled. "He's not...him."

Lewis nodded. "Okay. Then someone has taken Gracie Island on as a pet project this year. The radio tower. Now the trees. We have a benefactor."

"If they're related."

Lewis stood. "Of course they're related. Have you talked to Chris about the trees?"

"Just mine. He came by the house Friday night. He admits to leaving mine."

"Well, there you go."

Jasper shook his head. "That doesn't mean he's responsible for all of the others."

Lewis pointed at Jasper. "You need to relax and chill out a little. Just take the win. It's a gift. Be thankful."

Jasper sighed. "Trust me. I'm trying."

Chapter Fifteen

"I need to go make some bread."

It was the twenty-third, and the kids were getting anxious for Christmas to arrive. The antibiotics had cleared up Tucker's yearly ear infection, and he was back to his old rambunctious self.

Jasper was at his desk checking the office email when an alert from the weather service popped up. Once again, the NWS was announcing an unexpected snow storm heading in the direction of Gracie Island.

"Really? Do you really think we're going to buy it this time?"

When the phone rang, he knew it would either be his father or the mayor.

"Sheriff's office."

It was Thomas. "Hey, Jasper. Did you get the notification from the NWS?"

"Yeah. I'm looking at the report now."

"What do you think?"

"I think it's going to suddenly disappear like the last one."

"Hopefully. But I don't want to get caught unprepared. What can we do?"

"With a day's notice, not much. We don't have rock salt for slippery roads and sidewalks. Although I could ask Jake to bring some back on his last run."

"Alright. Let's do that."

Jasper laughed. "Hurricanes I know how to prepare for. Blizzards not so much. I'll send Lance and the guys to spread the word again. People might want to wrap their pipes to keep them from freezing. If the temperature drops, even without snow, we're going to have a lot of busted pipes."

"Can you prepare the station? And let the businesses in town know?"

"Yeah. Freezing temperatures we can prepare for."

"Better check with Steadman's and make sure they have lots of bottled water. You might ask Jake to bring back a few cases of that, too."

"Okay. I'll go talk to Jake."

"Thanks, Jasper."

"I'll let you know if I hear anything else."

Jasper hung up the phone and sighed, then got up from his desk and left his office.

Maisy smiled. "Are you taking off?"

"I need to talk to everyone on the street. The weather service just issued another blizzard warning."

"Oh my. Do think it'll actually snow this time?"

He shrugged. "No. But it might freeze. And busted pipes will put a damper on everyone's Christmas. Can you call Lance and have him round up some of the guys to talk to the residents in town?"

"Of course."

Jasper spent the next hour talking to all of the businesses in town. The men from the fire department would make sure the residents knew something might be coming. His last stop was The Sailor's Loft. He went inside and found Kat, Peg, and James sitting at a table. The rest of the restaurant was empty.

Jasper joined them and took a seat. "Why so slow?"

Kat smiled. "Two days until Christmas." She looked at James. "Also, your father came in and told everyone they needed to go home and prepare for a blizzard. Cleared the place right out."

James shrugged. "They have a right to know."

When Jasper's deputy, Quinn, came through the door, Jasper waved him over.

Quinn nodded at everyone. "I just got back from the mainland. Maisy told me to check in with you."

"The National Weather Service is predicting another snow storm."

"Dammit."

"Can you go ask Jake to bring rock salt and cases of water when he comes back from his next run?"

"How much of each?"

"All he can find. Within reason. I don't want him to be late. He hates to be late."

"Do you want me to go back with him? Help him out?"

"Do you mind? I know you just got home."

"No. It's fine."

"Okay. If you can do that, I'll hold down the fort here."

"Okay, chief. See you all later."

Kat stood up. "I need to go make some bread."

"Mom."

She waved at him. "I'm fine."

She headed for the kitchen and James looked at Jasper. "It's Christmas Eve tomorrow."

"Right." Jasper stood. "I'll go talk to her."

As much of a big deal as the family Thanksgiving dinner was every year. Christmas Eve was even more important to Kat. Christmas Eve was for the immediate family, which included Lewis, Sarah, and the kids, along with Maisy and Thomas, and Peg and Beryl. Quinn and Amy also came. Along with the Hannigans. It was at Kat and James' house with lots of food, exchanging of gifts, and singing around the piano. They'd been doing it for as long as Jasper could remember. And it wouldn't be Christmas without it.

He found Kat pouring flour into a bowl. "Mom."

She looked at him. "What if it really does snow?"

"Then we'll deal with it."

"What if nobody can get to the house?"

"Everyone but Poppie and I live close enough to walk if they have to."

She looked at him. "We can't have Christmas Eve without you."

He sat on a stool in front of her counter. "The chances of it actually snowing at all are really slim. And the chance it'd snow enough to stop the Bronco is microscopic."

"Do you promise?"

"I can't promise. Sometimes the impossible happens."

She set the flour down and added some sugar, salt, and oil to the flour, then mixed it in. "If you and the kids can't come in, then we'll wait until you can."

"It's going to be fine, Mom."

She added her prepared yeast to the flour mixture.

"One thing we do need to prepare for is our pipes freezing."

She nodded. "James and Beryl are taking care of that. Both here and at home."

"Good."

He watched her for a moment. "Can I help you with that?"

"Go wash your hands."

Jasper helped Kat for a while and continued to try to calm her down. But with Christmas Eve in danger of being interrupted, there wasn't a lot he could say to her. When they had four loaves of bread rising, he went to the sink and washed his hands again.

"I need to go."

"Thank you, honey."

"I don't want you to worry. Everything is going to be fine."

She nodded and kissed him on the cheek. "I hope you're right."

Jasper left the restaurant and returned to the station. He went to his office and called Poppie.

"Hello?"

"Hey. It's me, your husband."

"What's going on with the weather? I took the dogs out and it's cold. Different from normal Gracie Island in December cold."

"They're predicting another snow storm."

"You're kidding."

"Nope. I'm not too worried about getting snow. But the temperature dropping could be a problem. I'll be home soon to wrap our exterior pipes."

"Okay."

"Mom's freaking out about the possibility of snow."

"Is she afraid it's going to affect tomorrow night?"

"Yeah. I tried to talk with her about it while we made four loaves of bread."

"Oh my."

"Yeah. I'll bring one home with me."

"Okay, I'll see you soon."

Jasper had planned on getting home before dark, but he figured he should wait for Jake and Quinn to get back with the salt and the water. He drove to the marina and waited for the ferry, then he and Quinn hauled everything to the station.

"If we actually get snow, it won't be enough to stop the Bronco. So I'll be in at some point tomorrow, regardless of what happens tonight. But until I get in, you're in charge of distributing this to whoever needs it."

"Okay, Chief. No problem."

"Now I need to get home and check my pipes."

"Do you need help?"

"Nah. When we rebuilt the house, we put most everything underneath it or buried deep. The only exposed pipes are the outside faucets. Won't take me long."

"Okay. I'll see you tomorrow, then."

"Thanks, Quinn. Have a good night."

Before going home, Jasper went back to the Loft to check on Kat. There were only a few customers, and he found her in the kitchen. She'd be closed for the next two days, so she was preparing the kitchen for that.

"Hey, Mom."

"Hi, honey."

"I just came to check on you."

"I'm fine. I decided to go with the microscopic chance it'll snow too much for you to get into town."

"Good."

She handed him two loaves of bread. "Take these home with you. The boys love my bread."

Jasper smiled. "This boy loves your bread, too."

She gave him a hug. "I'll see you tomorrow."

He left her with no doubt in his mind that'd be true.

Jasper was dozing off when Poppie got into bed after giving Gracie her final feeding for the night. She'd be good until about six a.m. Poppie snuggled up next to him and started rubbing his thigh.

"Do you want to know another thing that'd be on my things I love about you list?"

"Sure."

"Your thighs."

Jasper rolled onto his back. "Seriously?"

"Yes. You have exceptional thighs."

"I'm not sure if I want to know how you know that. How many men's thighs have you caressed?"

She laughed. "I don't have to touch them to know they don't hold up to yours."

"Are we going to have another weird conversation? This time about men's thighs?"

"No. I just wanted you to know."

"Thanks for telling me."

She sat up and smiled at him.

He cocked his head. "What?"

"I can't wait any longer."

"I knew you wouldn't be able to wait until Christmas."

"I'm just so excited to give you your gift. I don't even care that it'll cost me a back rub."

"And a foot rub."

"That too."

He shook his head. "Go get it."

Poppie squealed and jumped off the bed before running to the closet. She dug around for a moment, then came back to the bed with a wrapped present. Jasper sat up and took it from her.

"So, any pre-story or explanation to go with it?"

"Open it."

Jasper removed the paper to reveal a painting. It was taken from an old photo he had of his great-great-grandfather standing in front of the newly built sheriff's station. The photo was black and white, but the painting was in color with the first Chief Deputy Goodspeed wearing his olive green uniform complete with his Mounty-style hat.

"Oh my gosh."

"It's great, right?"

"How'd you get this?"

"I have a friend in Boston who specializes in turning old photos into paintings."

He glanced at her. "Does this friend have great thighs?"

She laughed. "Yes, *she* does."

He looked at the painting again. "Other than you and the kids, this is the best gift I've ever gotten."

Poppie hugged him. "I'm glad you like it."

"I love it. I can't wait to hang it in my office." He looked at her. "Now I suppose you want yours."

"Yes, please."

"You still lost the bet."

"I know."

Jasper got out of bed and went to the dresser. He opened a drawer and took out a small wrapped package, then brought it back to the bed and sat down again. He held it out to her.

"Merry Christmas."

Poppie took the gift and started removing the paper. "What did you do?"

"Just open it."

She held the small box, then opened it and gasped. "Jasper? My gosh."

"Do you like it?"

"Is it their birthstones?"

"Yeah. And it's made to fit around your wedding rings."

"How did you get this made?"

He shrugged. "I have friends too."

She slipped on the ring with three gemstones representing the kids' birthstones. It was curved and fit around her engagement ring. She wiped away a tear. "Considering we weren't going to exchange gifts this year, we did pretty well."

Jasper grinned. "Yes, we did."

She studied the ring. "There's even room for…" She glanced at him. "I mean. If we decided to…"

He smiled. "Yes, honey, there's room for another stone. Maybe even two."

Chapter Sixteen

"What's poor Penny going to do?"

Jasper startled awake when Poppie shook him. "Jasper, you need to come see this."

He rolled over and buried his face in the pillow. "See what?"

"The snow."

"I'll see it at a decent hour."

She shook him again, and he rose onto an elbow and scowled at her. "Penelope?"

"Just come look."

He tossed the blankets back and followed her to the window.

"Shit." There was two feet of snow on the ground and it was still coming down. "That's not even possible."

"It's a Christmas miracle."

He returned to the bed and sat on the edge as he picked up the phone and dialed his parents' house.

James answered with, "I know. I see it."

"Dad? What the hell?"

"Never seen anything like it."

"I don't think I can even drive in this."

"You're right. You can't. And you'd be foolish to try. Just stay put. I've already talked with Quinn, Lance, and Mark. We're here in town. I'll walk over to the station and patch the phones through to the house. If there's a problem we can handle, we'll take care of it."

"Okay. Short of walking two miles to town in a couple feet of snow, there's not much I can do."

"I'll keep you updated."

"How's Mom taking it?"

"She's in the kitchen making more bread."

"Right. I'll check in with you in a while." He looked at Poppie, then laid back down on the bed. "Might as well get some more sleep."

As he was punching the pillow to make the perfect hollow for his head, the bedroom door was thrown open, and Jensen and Tucker came running in.

Jensen jumped on the bed. "Did you see it? Did you see the snow, Dad?"

Jasper rubbed his face and tucked a second pillow behind his head. "Yeah. I saw it."

"Isn't it cool?"

"It's pretty cool, all right."

Poppie lifted Tucker onto the bed and he crawled over to Jasper and patted his chest. "Snow."

Jasper nodded. "Lots and lots of snow."

Jensen bounced on his knees. "Can we go play in it? Can we go build a snowman and a snow fort?"

Poppie sat next to Jensen. "We need to eat breakfast first."

"Aww."

"Come on. Leave Dad alone and come eat some breakfast."

Jensen slid off the bed and followed Poppie out of the room.

Tucker smiled at Jasper. "Snow."

Jasper lifted him to the floor. "Breakfast."

Tucker ran out of the room and Jasper tried to get comfortable again, but he knew it was no use. He had snowmen and a snow fort in his near future. He got up, got dressed, and went into the kitchen.

Poppie had the boys at the table and they were eating excitedly. He poured himself a cup of coffee and took a muffin from a box on the counter.

"I'm going to go walk the mutts."

Poppie looked at him. "What's poor Penny going to do?"

"I'll find a spot under a tree or next to the house. I'll clear a spot for her if I have to." He took another sip of coffee, then set his cup down and picked up Penny. With the dog in one hand and his muffin in the other, he opened the front door and let the two big dogs out. They ran through the door, then both stopped abruptly when they saw the snow.

Jasper laughed. He set his muffin down, tucked Penny into his coat, then picked up Blackjack. Sam would have no trouble navigating the deep snow. But Blackjack had a bad hip. Jasper figured there would be less snow closer to the water. He stepped off the porch into thigh-deep snow and made his way slowly for the beach. As he'd hoped, the closer he got to the water, the less snow there was. But it still covered the ground, which made for an interesting picture. He watched as the waves crashed on sand that had a light layer of snow on it. After a moment, he set Blackjack down, then took Penny from his jacket and put her on the snow-covered sand. She didn't appreciate it and she tried to sit on his boot.

"Go pee. Then I'll pick you up again."

Penny hesitated and whined for a moment, then ran off to do her business. Jasper gave the dogs twenty minutes, then took them back to the house, following the path he'd made through the snow. Blackjack was able to navigate it on his own, following close behind Jasper.

When he went inside, he headed for the kitchen with his uneaten muffin. He drank some coffee, then looked at Poppie.

"Really cold out there."

She looked at his wet pants. "And also wet?"

"That, too."

"The kids are going to get soaked."

"I'll go build up the fire."

Jasper had the fire going and was trying to stand close enough to dry his pants when Poppie came in the room. She went and stood by him.

"Are we going to miss the Christmas Eve party?"

"I don't think the snow is going to magically disappear so we can drive in."

"And we won't see Lewis, Sarah, and the kids tomorrow?"

He put his arms around her. "We'll see them as soon as we can. In the meantime, we need to make a special Christmas with the kids without all of the family around."

"Can we have a second Christmas with family when the snow clears?"

"As long as we don't have to give the kids more presents. I think you overdid it this year."

Jensen came in and put his hands on his hips. "When can we go play in the snow?"

"Hold on. I'm warming your mother up."

Poppie kissed him, then stepped away. "First off, we need to get dressed super warm."

"Okay."

"It's really wet and cold. And when you get too cold, you need to come in and warm up."

"I won't get cold."

"Yes. You will. But once you come in and get warm and dry, you can go back out."

"Are you coming?"

"I'll come when I put Gracie down for her nap."

Tucker ran into the room and stopped next to Jensen. "Snow."

Jasper frowned at him. "Snow, please, Dad?"

Tucker returned his father's frown, then said, "Snow." After a moment, he added, "Dad."

Jasper laughed. "Close enough."

After Poppie got the boys bundled up, Jasper took them out to the porch. He picked up Tucker. "Okay, Jensen, follow me. We're going to go down by the beach. It's not as deep there."

Jasper stepped into the path he'd made with the dogs and Jensen followed close behind him. When they got to the beach, Tucker wiggled to get down.

"Okay, here you go."

While the boys ran around in the snow, Jasper started clearing the snow from the sand, forming a large circle. Jensen came over to watch him.

"What are you doing?"

"I figure we can build a big old fire here and not have to go inside to get warmed up?"

"Yay. Can we roast marshmallows, too?"

"Sure."

"Hotdogs?"

"If we have some."

Jensen jumped up and down, then went to join Tucker, who was picking up handfuls of snow and throwing it at the incoming waves. After about thirty minutes, Poppie came down to join them. She had Gracie in her arms.

"Seems Gracie wants to see the snow, too."

"If you've got these guys for a minute, I'm going to go get some firewood from the porch."

"Oh, good idea."

"I come up with one once in a while."

Jasper made his way to the house and loaded up with firewood. He made two more trips, then started a fire with kindling and newspaper. Once it was going, he added some of the dry firewood.

Poppie came and stood next to the fire with Jasper and they watched the boys playing in the snow. "I think they like it."

Jasper looked up at the cloudy sky. The snow was still falling. "I'm glad they get to experience it. It may be their first and last time. As long as they stay on the island."

She tucked a blanket tighter around Gracie. "And Gracie missed it." She looked at Jasper. "How upset is Kat going to be over this?"

"We'll have lots of bread when we all get together."

Jensen ran up to them. "Can we build a snowman now?"

"Of course."

Poppie stayed by the fire with Gracie and watched Jasper and the boys build a giant snowman. When it was finished, they decided to build another. By the time they were done, they'd built a whole snow family with mom, dad, two kids, and a tiny baby snowman for Gracie. It was adorable.

When they were finished, they came to the fire to get warm.

Jensen looked at Jasper. "Can we have hotdogs now?"

"Sure. I'm hungry."

Poppie patted Jensen on the head. "Let me go put Gracie to bed and I'll bring out the hotdogs and buns."

"Yay."

Tucker clapped his hands. "Yay."

She left them by the fire and followed the cleared path to the house. Since the snow was still falling, Jasper's trail had started filling in again. But it was still fairly easy to walk down. She went into the house and put Gracie in her crib, then put the baby monitor in her coat pocket.

She went to the phone to call Sarah.

"Hello?"

"Sarah, it's me."

"Poppie, is it bad out there?"

"Yeah. At least two feet and still coming down."

"You're stranded out there?"

"It would seem so."

"We could walk to Kat's. But I'm pretty sure she wants to postpone until you guys can make it."

"Hopefully by tomorrow. I can't see this lasting past tomorrow. What a weird fluke this is."

"Yeah. I've never seen it snow like this and neither have my parents."

"Well, we are embracing the snow. Jasper and the boys have built several snowmen. And we're about to cook hotdogs over the bonfire Jasper lit on the beach."

"Good. I'm sure the boys are loving it. Maybe they won't be too upset to miss Christmas Eve with the family."

"I'm sure they'll miss it. They just haven't thought about it yet."

"Okay. I'll let you get back out there to them. I love you. And call me later."

"I will."

She ended the call and went to the kitchen to gather hotdogs, buns, chips, and marshmallows. Along with a bottle of mustard and a roll of paper towels. She brought two bottles of juice for the boys and a bottle of beer for Jasper. She took a water for herself. She put it all into a bag and went back outside.

Jasper met her halfway down the path and took the bag of stuff from her. He set it by the fire, then went to clear the snow from the wooden bench. He dragged it near the fire and the boys sat down on it. Poppie sat between them.

Jasper was the official hotdog roaster, and he cooked dogs for the boys, then one for himself and Poppie.

Jensen looked up at Jasper. "So when are we going to Grandma and Grandpa's?"

Chapter Seventeen

"I think this is a PJ kind of day."

Once Jensen heard they wouldn't be able to go to Christmas Eve with the family, he lost interest in the snow. Jasper put the fire out with snow and sand, then they all returned to the house. Jensen went straight to his room.

Poppie sighed. "I didn't think it'd hit him that hard."

Jasper put a hand on her shoulder. "I'll go talk to him."

Jasper found Jensen sitting on his bed. He sat down next to him and nudged him.

"Sorry kid. But it's just a delay. We'll have our family Christmas as soon as the snow melts enough for me to drive us to town."

Jensen fell back onto the bed. "It's never going to go away."

"It will, son. You know we never get snow here. This won't last." He laid next to Jensen. "But in the meantime, we can still have fun while we're waiting for it to melt."

"Are they having Christmas without us?"

"No, honey. They're waiting for us."

"How can we have fun while we're waiting?"

"Hmm. We could make some Christmas decorations. Or string popcorn. We can color some more Christmas sharks."

"What's string popcorn?"

"It's stringing popcorn on some thread. Then you hang it on the Christmas tree."

Jensen turned his head and looked at Jasper. "How about we open presents?"

"No. We can't do that until tomorrow."

"Can Santa get to us in all this snow?"

Jasper raised onto an elbow. "Of course. Santa lives at the North Pole. He's used to the snow. Plus, he has flying reindeer. Snow isn't a problem."

"But isn't he stuck at Sam's place without his sleigh?"

"I'm sure Santa will figure out how to get his job done. He hasn't missed a Christmas yet."

Jensen sighed. "What other fun things are there to do?"

Poppie was at the door. "We can make cookies."

Jensen sat up. "Can we eat them?"

"Within reason, yes."

He slid off the bed. "Let's do that."

"Okay, you need to change out of your wet things first." She handed him a pair of pajamas.

"I get to wear my PJs?"

"Yes. I think this is a PJ kind of day."

He ran out of the room to go to the bathroom, as Poppie sat next to Jasper. "You'll come help, right?"

"Sure. I just need to call Dad and see how things are going in town."

Poppie kissed him. "Okay. You need to change, too."

"Can I wear my PJs?"

"I insist that you do."

She left to go help Jensen and Jasper went to their bedroom to get changed. He put on a pair of green plaid pajama pants and a tan thermal shirt, then called his parents' house."

Kat answered. "Hello?"

"Hey, Mom."

"Oh, honey. How bad is it out there?"

"Not bad. Jensen's disappointed about missing tonight. But we're trying to keep him occupied."

"Bless his heart. Is it still snowing? It stopped here."

"It stopped here, too. But it's not melting yet."

"Well, I called everyone and they're all in agreement that we wait until you can get into town."

"Thanks, Mom. We'll get there as soon as we can."

"I know. Give Poppie and the boys our love."

"Will do. Love you, Mom."

"I love you more."

He talked to James next, and it seemed everything was as good as it could be in town after a freak snowstorm. Everyone was lying low and staying home. It was good news, and it made Jasper feel a little less useless being stuck at home.

After talking with James, Jasper joined the family in the kitchen. He looked at the boys, who were both in pajamas, then at Poppie.

"Um...seems like one of us is still dressed."

She smiled. "I'll be right back."

Poppie returned shortly in red pajamas with Christmas trees on them and a red pull-over sweater. "Better?"

"Perfect."

They spent the afternoon making, decorating, and eating cookies. Then Poppie made some popcorn and Jasper showed Jensen how to put it on a string. They made several strands and hung them on the tree.

When dinnertime rolled around, the boys weren't hungry, having eaten cookies and popcorn all afternoon. So Poppie settled them down in their room with a DVD, and she and Jasper sat on the couch in the living room. Gracie was on the floor on a blanket, entertaining herself with her feet.

Jasper put his arm around Poppie. "Pretty good day considering the once in a lifetime snow storm."

"We'll get to see everyone tomorrow, right?"

"I hope so."

They sat for a few minutes, enjoying the quiet house and the warm fire. When Jasper heard something, he sat up. "Do you hear that?"

"I don't hear anything. What is it?"

"Bells. Like...sleigh bells."

Poppie listened for a moment, then they both got up and went to the window as a wagon pulled up out front of the house, pulled by six of Chris' eight reindeer. The other two were tied to the rear of the wagon. And they all had bells on the harnesses. Chris waved at them, then climbed down from the wagon and made his way to the porch.

Jasper opened the door. "Chris?"

"Merry Christmas."

"What are you doing here? And where did the wagon come from?"

"It was in Sam's shed."

Jasper had been in Sam's shed and he didn't remember seeing a wagon. "Well, come on in."

"Okay, just while you're getting ready to go."

"Go where?"

"To the family Christmas Eve party, of course. Go bundle up those kids. It's cold out there."

Jasper shook his head. "You're taking us to my mom's house?"

"Yes. Of course."

Jasper looked at Poppie. "Go get the kids ready." He looked at his pajamas." I'll get dressed."

When Jasper returned to the living room, Chris was holding Gracie and walking her around the room. "She got a bit fussy once you and Poppie both left."

"Are you sure the reindeer can pull us all?"

"Oh sure. Not a problem."

Jensen ran out of the bedroom and hugged Chris' leg. "I knew you'd come to save the day."

Chris laughed. "Are you ready to go, young man?"

"Yes, sir."

Poppie came out carrying Tucker. "Should we call Kat and let her know we're coming?"

Jasper smiled. "Let's surprise her. I will call Lewis though and have him call everyone else."

He went to the phone and dialed Lewis' number.

"Merry Christmas."

"Hey, Lewis."

"How's it going out there?"

"Well, we're catching a ride, actually. Can you call everyone except my parents, and tell them we're on our way, and have them meet up at the Loft? Then wait for us there."

"Sure. You're not driving, are you?"

"No. We'll see you soon."

They all went outside and Jasper lifted the kids into the wagon that was filled with straw bales to sit on. He helped Poppie and Gracie in, then climbed up next to Chris.

Chris smiled at him. "Are you ready?"

"Let's go."

Chris circled the reindeer in the driveway, then followed the path he'd made on the way in. Jasper shook his head. "I can't believe you came all the way from Sam's place to come and get us."

"It's Christmas Eve."

"Yeah. It sure is."

It took about thirty minutes to get into town, and when they pulled in front of The Sailor's Loft, everyone was there waiting for them. Jasper jumped down.

"Chris and the boys saved the day."

Lewis put his kids and Sarah in the wagon, and the rest of them followed behind it. Halfway to Kat and James' house, Chris started singing a Christmas song. Everyone joined in and Kat and James heard them coming because they were on the porch when Chris pulled the wagon up to their house.

Jasper and Lewis helped the kids and Poppie and Sarah down, and everyone headed inside. Jasper looked up at Chris.

"Come on inside, Chris."

Chris smiled. "I've got a couple of things for you." He handed Jasper a present. "This was something on Jensen's list. Probably something he never figured he'd get." He then picked up a Christmas tin. "Some cookies for your party. And..." He took a folded piece of paper from his pocket. "This is for Kat. It's my cookie recipe." He winked. "For her eyes only. It's a family secret."

Jasper looked at the writing on the wrapped present. It was the same neat printing he'd seen on the Christmas tree list.

"I'd really like you to come in for a while, Chris."

"I've love to. But I've got to get back."

"To an empty house? Come join us."

"I've got things to do."

Jasper cocked his head. "Chris, I've got to know."

Chris laughed. "You already know, Jasper." He whistled, and the reindeer started moving. "Thanks for sharing your island with me."

"Will we see you again?"

"Of course. I'll be back next year."

Chris waved and Jasper watched until he lost sight of the wagon in the dark and could no longer hear the bells. Then he went inside.

Poppie came up to him. "Is Chris joining us?"

"No. The man says he's got things to do."

"Jasper?"

"Come on. Let's join the family."

"But?"

He kissed her. "Merry Christmas Penelope. Just take the gift and be thankful."

More Books By Leigh Fenty

The Three Oaks Ranch Series
Memories Of You
The Good Son
The Wayward Son
Little Sis
The Carmichael Series
Deacon
Tobias
Abligale
Tanner
The Christmas Wedding
Faith's Journal
The Gracie Island Series

The Deputy
The Best Woman
The Chief
The Family Man
The Visitor

About the Author

Leigh spends her days with cute, sexy guys. Unfortunately, they're on paper. But still, not a bad way to spend your day. She also writes about strong, independent women, who can hold their own against these irresistible guys. She's not a pure romance writer, because she breaks the rules a bit. But that's the fun part. Leigh's stories have adventure, family relationships, and the struggles life throws at you sometimes. But boy always meets girl. They tussle a bit while they figure out what they really want. Then find their happily ever after. Even if it's not what they thought it was going to be.

Made in United States
Orlando, FL
20 May 2024

47068644R00085